A Pure Flame

A Pure Flame

Rebecca Gray

Cavalier Publishing

Cover Painting by Patience Anders
All Rights Reserved
Cover Design by Elizabeth Jaxon
Photo by Jim Ream

Published by Cavalier Publishing

Typesetting services by BOOKOW.COM

This, my first novel, is dedicated to my parents, who were both writers in their own right. They modeled for me the idea that it is never too late to start something new and that learning is always an exciting and worthwhile adventure.

Acknowledgments

I am forever grateful to my husband, Greg, who never laughed at me for loving romance novels and who helped me brainstorm plot elements whenever I needed it.

Thanks to my daughters, Elizabeth and April, who inspired me with their own love of writing, and to my son, Noah, who encourages me in all my interests.

Thank you to all my friends and beta-readers: Patience Anders, Susan Boston, Elizabeth Jaxon, Greg Jaxon, Beth Koos, Alice Muciek, Kristin Oakley, Dawn Root, and Jennifer Stevenson, who read and critiqued the several different versions of this novel. It is much better for your efforts.

A special thank you goes to Patience Anders for the many hours she spent creating the artwork for my cover, and to her lovely daughter, Autumn, for modeling for the initial image.

I especially appreciate Jennifer Stevenson, without whose prodding and constant tutelage I would never have even begun this project, much less finished.

I am grateful for my friend, Cindy Gaddis, who commiserated with me, and gave me my own advice right back again at just the right time.

Thanks also goes to Becky Akers for encouraging me in starting my new career, and helping me think through some of the details of my character's academic life.

"Claudia's moral compass is pointed at 'confused.' She has learned self-respect since she left home. Now she's back home, where she can't seem to do anything right. I got totally caught up in Claudia's fight for independence from her well-to-do family rules and her bossy lawyer father. Then her working-class high-school boyfriend came along. . . I'm a sucker for working class heroes! An emotional ride!"

— Jennifer Stevenson, author of The Brass Bed series, and many others

CHAPTER 1

Claudia rolled her chair back and pushed the hair from her eyes. She had been studying the pottery shards under the microscope for so long that her eyes were not focusing any more. She had to take a break, even though she had finally reached the stage where the pieces were literally coming together. She stretched her back and rolled her neck around trying to loosen up. She was relieved when her advisor in the anthropology program handed her a cup of coffee and sat down beside her for a chat.

"I've been reading over your paper since you completed your last round of edits," she began, "and I think you'll be ready to send it to a publisher once you've added in these last few figures. You're a good writer."

Claudia flushed at the praise. "Thank you so much, Dr. Spencer. You've taught me well."

"We could start talking about your next project if you'd like. This one won't take too much longer. If you get started on your research during the break, you will have a good head start before your graduate classes begin in the fall."

"I was hoping to talk to you about that! I have several ideas of my own, but I'd also like to hear yours. I have a few finals to take next week, but I think after that, I'll be ready to launch into work again."

"You won't be going home for a while?"

"I wasn't going to. I should talk to my parents and see if they have any plans."

Donna Spencer smiled. "I wish I'd been able to meet your parents, Claudia. I would have liked to tell them what a pleasure it's been to have you in my lab. Not many students are so dedicated to their work so early in their college career."

Claudia averted her eyes for a moment, and then she smiled and said, "I would have loved for them to meet you too, and to know what I've been doing all these years. It's just been hard for them to travel this far. They are very busy."

"I'm sure that's true. Will they be coming for your graduation?"

"I sent them the invitation. They haven't mentioned yet whether they think they can make it."

"Why don't you go home and give them a call. You should quit for the day anyway."

"Uh, okay. I'll go do that."

* * *

Walking to her apartment, Claudia reminisced about her first year at college. She had signed up for her first anthropology class, during the fall semester. Even though it was originally meant to be just a filler class, she became fascinated by the subject matter. Without consulting her parents, she declared it her major, and began to woo Dr. Spencer. She started by hanging out in the teaching assistant's office, asking questions that had nothing to do with the next test or assignment, but about subjects that her curiosity had led her to from a topic discussed during the previous day's lecture.

When the TA realized that he couldn't answer Claudia's questions anymore and that she wasn't going to quit, he sent her along to the professor's office. Claudia enjoyed her regular talks with Dr. Spencer. They began each meeting by discussing Claudia's questions, and then Claudia would leave with a reading list that she could pursue if she had the time and was interested. She always came back having read through everything and, often, having also used the references list at the end of an article to guide her way through more of the literature.

Dr. Spencer realized what a prize student she had on her hands and encouraged Claudia in her explorations. Soon, Claudia was working in her professor's laboratory, conducting research and helping to write papers that came out of that research. Her senior thesis was the culmination of her four years of reading and represented an original study that she had designed and carried out herself.

Claudia knew that Dr. Spencer thought a great deal of her. In fact, she had urged Claudia to stay for another year at least, to work on publishing her senior paper, but also, to start work on a graduate degree. With her guidance and a glowing letter of recommendation, Claudia had made out the application to the graduate program and was accepted.

When she shared the news with her friends, they were excited for her, just as she would have wished them to be. But, her mother, instead of being proud, met her announcement with silence. Her father wasn't home the day she told her mother on the phone, and she never did hear how he had reacted to her being accepted to graduate school.

Letting herself into the apartment, she greeted her roommate and closed herself up in her room. She nervously dialed the telephone.

"Hello."

"Mom, is that you?"

"Yes, Claudia. We're just sitting down to dinner. Is there something important?"

"Uh, I was wondering…"

"What is it dear?"

"You know I'm graduating next week? Did you get my invitation?"

"Yes, of course we got it. I'm so sorry. Your father has an important case and can't take any time off."

"Th—that's okay. Well, I was also wondering, if there is any need for me to come home this spring. I have a lot of research to do…"

"Oh, graduate school. Yes, you did mention that. I think your father has different plans for you."

"What do you mean? What plans?"

Claudia, waited in alarm while her parents conferred quietly away from the telephone. Suddenly her father's voice came on the line.

"Claudia? Graduate school is out of the question. It's time for you to come home."

"What? Why?"

"I'm afraid you forgot. The agreement was for you to go to college for four years and then come home. I can't support you any longer."

"Agreement? What agreement? I don't remember agreeing to anything."

"That's all *I* agreed to. Of course, you don't remember. You just assumed that you could do whatever you wanted to do with my money, and now you want to stretch it out as long as possible. But no, that's not the way it's going to work. It's time for you to pack up and come home. When is your last final? This week, right? I'll expect you home the day after that."

"But, graduation, Dad!"

"It's a waste of time and money. Since we can't be there, there's no need for you to be either."

"Wh...?"

"I can't speak about this any longer. We're just sitting down for dinner. We'll see you next week and talk about what you should do next."

Claudia hung up the phone slowly. Tears rolled, unnoticed, down her cheeks. Almost in a daze, she headed back to the lab to announce that she would be leaving in just a few days.

* * *

Claudia sipped her coffee and hummed determinedly to the car radio. The Taurus's engine was making a knocking sound, and she was trying to ignore it. She glanced at the mile gauge. Still 120 miles to go, and she absolutely did not want to have to find a mechanic halfway home. No new lights on the dashboard. She willed it to be nothing. At least the traffic was pretty light on Route 43 so she let her mind wander.

It had been hard for her to return the key to her campus apartment that morning. Her roommate, Anne, had already departed on the early morning flight to the West Coast. She would be coming back after a two-month-long internship, so she had left most of her things behind. But Claudia's room was empty—completely cleaned out—ready to receive its next occupant. She had worked hard to leave the room, and also the entire apartment, in pristine condition, but even so, she was surprised at how little evidence there was of the years that she spent in that space, reading, studying, and dreaming. She had hung pictures on the walls, filled the shelves with her books, and made the space reflect exactly who she was. But now it was empty, a blank slate. The emptiness spread until it invaded her soul as she closed the door for the last time, filled up the gas tank, and drove out of town.

The drive had been uneventful so far. But it was long, and Claudia just wanted it to be over. Interstate 90 was the same as far as the eye could see, though the scenery in each state differed. New York was the most beautiful, with its rolling hills and lush vegetation. Now, as she was nearing Chicago, the land was getting flatter and the industrial parks more numerous, with their smoke stacks billowing black clouds into the air.

Claudia could feel her anxiety level rising. She began to worry about what she would find at home. Her parents would undoubtedly expect her to start looking for a job. But with only a bachelor's in anthropology, she didn't know what kind of job she would be suited for. She had called home again to argue for being allowed to stay, but her father had put his foot down on her "playing around in the dirt," as he put it. Her mother, as usual, had backed him up and turned a deaf ear to her daughter's protests.

Claudia was angry, more at herself than at her parents. Why hadn't she stood up for herself? Why hadn't she just told her parents off and found some way to continue her studies without their blessing? She was not a meek person normally in the outside world, but when her parents were involved suddenly she became the oldest daughter who was always looking for approval.

Getting it from her father had always seemed like an impossible goal. Claudia could usually win over her mother, though, by helping out a lot around the house. She had already gotten a clue to the problems she was expected to solve as soon as she got home.

"I am at my wit's end! Zoë is never home! I think she has some bad friends. She might even be doing drugs. What must it look like to your father's partners when he can't even control his youngest child? Things like this never happened when your brother was in high school."

Benjamin, the oldest, had never done anything wrong, at least as far as her parents were concerned. Zoë was another story though.

"Mom, I don't know that she'll even talk to me. I haven't seen her in ages. And I'm supposed to be looking for a job."

"Well, when you're not working, try to spend some time with her. Think of something for the two of you to do together."

She furrowed her brow now as she thought about her sister. Zoë was five years younger than she was, so even when Claudia was still at home, the two sisters hadn't run in the same circles, though they always got along well. On the other hand, Claudia had been away at college and barely knew her sister any more. She was looking forward to renewing their relationship. There was something special about sisters, and she missed hers. Still, she felt uncomfortable being asked to interfere in Zoë's life. She'd rather become part of it without having an ulterior motive.

Hey! Good song! She turned up the volume on the radio, "Let it be, let it be-e, let it be-e-e, let it be!"

She sighed. The miles stretched on. They were going by awfully slowly even as her destination was growing closer and closer. She was ready to be done with the driving.

Her coffee was getting cold. She had added as much cream as she could fit into the cup before she left the gas station where she had filled the gas tank a second time. It was bad enough coffee when she first poured it, but now it was noticeably bitter. It did give her something to do though while she counted down the miles toward home. Ninety-three to go.

She wondered what it would be like at home. Her current plan was to find a job and her own place, but as of yet, she hadn't decided what kind of work she'd look for. She was going to have to just see what was available and hope for the best.

Claudia had dreamed of finishing her education so that she could get a prestigious job in a museum, maybe even in New York or Chicago. Or maybe she could go into academia and inspire other promising students like herself. Or even live far away and do primary research in Africa, like Mary Leakey. She had always thought it would be very exciting to be at a major dig, discovering bones of humankind's distant ancestors.

But here she was, driving home with all of her possessions in the trunk of the car. She was heading back to her childhood, and she dreaded what she would find. She punched the buttons on the radio, looking for another recognizable song to hum along with.

Her thoughts drifted to someone she had tried to forget and now couldn't avoid thinking about—Jeff Gordon. He still lived in Carlsburg, where they both grew up and where they had fallen in love and then somehow fallen out of love just before she left town to go away to college. She hadn't spoken to him or heard from him in all that time, and she didn't know if he ever even thought of her. But her friend Andi had told her recently that Jeff was still there.

"Claudia, he's still gorgeous, and I know he's still single!"

Claudia didn't want to hear news like that. She had enough to think about. She didn't want him on her mind while she was busy pounding the pavement looking for a fulltime job!

It was nearly dinnertime when she finally pulled up her parents' driveway. She leaned back in the seat and closed her eyes for a moment, exhausted after fourteen hours of watching the road and worrying about the sound in her automobile's engine. During the last two hours she had been looking into the sun, or rather trying to avoid looking into the sun, so now she really was tired. She reached into the back seat for her purse, got out of the car, and stretched her long legs before walking up the steps to the front door. It was locked. She rang, but no one came to the door. She walked around the house and tried the back door before she finally sat down on the step to dig through her purse for her house key. Letting herself in, she blinked and waited for her eyes to adjust to the darkness.

She moved slowly through the quiet house. It didn't seem like home any more. She had been back only for a few short visits for Christmas or spring break throughout her college years, but now hadn't been home in a year and a half. Nothing seemed familiar to her. Was this a new sofa? Was the living room always painted yellow? It looked as if her mother had totally redecorated the house in her absence. But her mother had always liked change for its own sake. It would have surprised Claudia to find things too much the same.

Suddenly she heard a door slam, and a light went on somewhere. Her mother's voice was calling, "Claudia, are you here?"

Lights started to come on and Claudia began to feel better. She smiled and followed the sounds her mother was making in the kitchen where she was setting sacks of groceries on the counter. "Would you run out to the car and bring in the other bags, dear? I'll get dinner started."

"Sure, Mom," Claudia said, pausing a moment, thinking that her mother might offer some sort of greeting or welcome home. Nothing came, so she went on outside. For Pete's sake! Couldn't her mother have hugged her or something? She took a deep breath. *That's no way to start out. It's not like I was gone against my will. She knew where I was. We've been in touch all this time. What did I expect, anyway?* The thought was so upsetting she almost forgot what she had gone outside for, until the grocery bags peeking out of the open truck of the car caught her eye.

When she came in, balancing the last three bags on her hip, her mother was already pulling out pots and pans, pouring water into one and measuring olive oil into another. She was focused on her work, so Claudia busied herself by putting away the groceries and setting the table. She scowled in spite of her efforts to be pleasant.

Before the two women finished their tasks, voices could be heard from the front of the house, and Claudia's father and brother walked in. They were deep in conversation.

"I still think you should have told Dr. Anton that you were ready to take that exam, Benjamin. You have to keep your lead in the class if you want the best position next year."

"I know you keep saying that, Dad, but I'll be ready soon. I want a perfect score. I'm still studying all the literature behind the treatments for each of the diseases covered this semester, and I want to have it down cold. I'm almost there. Really, stop worrying."

"Well, how soon will you be ready? Isn't the deadline for the Yale internship coming up fast?"

"I still have time, Dad. The deadline isn't until next month. I'll be ready in time."

"Okay, Roger," Claudia's mother broke into their conversation, "you and Benjamin move into the living room with this conversation. And take Claudia with you. I'll have dinner ready soon."

Claudia's father started, as though he only just realized that he and Benjamin were not the only people present. Then he suddenly plastered a large jovial smile on his face. He gave his wife a peck on the cheek, and opening the door, he ushered his two eldest offspring into the next room. Always the good host, he showed them both to the comfortable sofa, while he settled himself in an easy chair.

"So, Claudia, you're home! How was the drive?"

Claudia blinked. "It went smoothly. My car is making a new noise. I was worried, but it never got worse, and well, I made it anyway."

"Well, we'll have to get that looked at. I'll give you the number of my mechanic, and you can call him in the morning. And how were your finals? Do you have your grades yet for the last semester?"

Claudia saw that though he was looking her way, her brother wasn't paying attention to the conversation. She tried to catch his eye but he didn't respond.

"Umm." She turned back to her father. "Finals went very well, Dad, but I can't get a full transcript until the middle of next month.

I'm sure my grades are good though." Her voice trailed away as she saw the stern expression on her father's face.

"I wouldn't be overconfident if I were you. That's how the professional world sorts the winners from the losers." He smiled as he spoke, but his eyes were hard as his gaze moved from Claudia to her brother. He seemed to lose interest in her and her achievements or lack thereof. "Your brother is also finishing up his classes. He has to take his qualifying exams soon to continue in the program. He'll be studying hard, so don't bother him when he's in his room. He'll have to concentrate very hard and cannot be distracted."

It amazed her that she could come home after living independently and interacting with others as an adult for four years and within ten minutes be made to feel petulant and childish. She tried to shrug it off. "I wouldn't dream of bothering Benjamin. I'll be busy myself. I will be looking for work, you know."

"Well, that's a good idea." His glance went from one of his children to the other. "I wish you luck. It might not be as easy as you think, though. This economy has been particularly unfriendly to the unskilled labor market."

Claudia's eyes widened. She was speechless. Her father had been the one to insist that she come home before her education was finished. And now he saw her as part of the "unskilled labor market." She was so angry that she was afraid to say anything else. If she did, she might be unleashing a flood of words she would never be able to take back.

"Ummm, I think I'll go see what I can do to help Mom." She got up and walked back through the kitchen door, conscious that the confidence she had attempted to display had just drained completely away. She hoped that her shoulders were not drooping noticeably. She heard her brother's voice as she closed the door on the scene.

"Did I tell you, Dad, Professor Bingham was very pleased with my lab reports for the study I did last week on the…"

"Hi Mom, can I help with anything?" Her mother was just sliding a casserole into the oven. Claudia looked into the dining room and saw that the table was already set and the candles lit.

"Why no, dear, it's not necessary. I have things all under control."

"Well then, I'll start unloading my car."

"That's fine, dear. Just take your things into your old room. I've made you a little space in the closet and emptied some of the drawers again. That should be enough for you."

Claudia reached the driveway when tears of anger and frustration began to come. She had been away at school living on her own, had made friends and felt like she belonged—as if she were intelligent in her own right. But that life was over. Her friends had scattered to their own respective homes. She had convinced herself to be optimistic about being back, but now she realized that coming home meant regressing to her former powerless self. She opened the trunk and dragged out the first big box. There wasn't going to be enough space for all this stuff in her old bedroom, especially if her mother's things were in the closet. Did she not expect Claudia to stay long? That was odd considering she had been ordered to come home. And the books and kitchen items would only be redundant in her parents' house. She had to get going on the job search so she could move out as soon as possible. But how to begin?

After she had trudged up and down the stairs to her bedroom several times, the car still looked full. She would have to carve out some storage space for herself down in the basement, and just leave the boxes closed up. But before she could go outside for another load, her mother's voice called them all to dinner. Claudia met her brother at the bathroom door as they both headed in to wash their hands. She tried to catch his eye, wishing for some sympathy or understanding. He looked away. They silently took their seats at the table.

"Claudia says she is going to look for a job," her father announced as he helped himself to the salad. All eyes turned toward Claudia as if on cue.

"Yes," she said hesitantly, looking around the table. "I'd like to find my own apartment too. I'm used to living on my own now."

"Well, that's nice, dear," her mother said. "Would you take some of the casserole and pass it on, please?"

Claudia spooned some of the chicken and broccoli onto her plate and handed it to her brother, who finally looked at her directly.

"What kind of job do you want, Claudia? Maybe I can ask around the department for any open secretarial positions." He glanced quickly at their father before turning back to his food.

"It's nice of you to offer, Benjamin." She took a bite of chicken and chewed it slowly. "I'd really like to look for something related to my degree, though. Why don't you hold off on that for now."

Out of the corner of her eye she saw the doubtful glance her father directed toward her mother.

Her mother pursed her lips, then said, "Honey, what kind of job would that be? I mean, anthropology isn't really one of the most marketable degrees in the world, is it?"

Her father put on his jovial voice again, "Actually, Claudia, anywhere you are dealing with people would use your degree, don't you think? I'm sure you can't be too choosy in this economy."

"Well, I suppose…"

"But, I was thinking that you should come apply for a secretarial position at the firm. It would be a good job for you."

She looked helplessly at her brother, who suddenly found his salad very troublesome as he poked at the lettuce with his fork. She fumed inwardly. If she had any idea how to go about searching for a job herself, she would argue, but she really didn't. She started concentrating on her own salad.

Taking a tomato on her fork, she dipped it into the dressing. She knew there was no arguing with her father. Roger Gilmore, being one of the foremost trial lawyers in the region, would often take the opposite side of whoever he was talking with just to practice his debating skills. He always won. Her mother would not be any help either. Annette Gilmore always supported her husband in everything he did or said.

Claudia looked around the table, wishing she could think of another topic of conversation. "Where's Zoë, Mom? I thought she'd be here."

Her father harrumphed, but before her mother could open her mouth to speak, they heard the front door slam.

CHAPTER 2

Jeff Gordon was just finishing up the wiring for all the outlets in the kitchen of the demo house that was going up in the new subdivision on the edge of town. There would still be a lot of testing to do tomorrow, but at least he was ready to close up for today. Before putting his tools back in their proper places, he wiped down each one with the chamois cloth hanging from his belt. It was this tendency to take such care in his work that made him one of the most sought after electricians in Carlsburg.

Climbing down the ladder from the front entrance to what would eventually become someone's front yard, he wiped his forehead with his sleeve. It would feel good to get a shower and sit down for a while in front of the television.

"Hey, Jeff! Where're you going?"

Oh no. Stewart Mills was a hard guy to put off. Jeff walked quickly, trying to ignore Stewart, but knowing it probably wouldn't work. It didn't.

"Let's stop at Trixie's, Jeff." Stewart caught up with him on the way down the hill toward their cars. "I could really use a beer, and Andi doesn't get off work for another couple of hours."

"Hey, you're really seeing her a lot, aren't you, Stewart?" Jeff tried to change the subject as he threw his toolbox into the back of his van.

"I sure am. She's pretty fun and doesn't get too serious on you, you know?"

Jeff shook his head. "Someday you're going to want to get serious. You don't want to die all alone, do you?"

"There's time for that. Now I'm just having fun. Speaking of which, Andi tells me her friend Claudia Gilmore is coming back to town this weekend. She says you two used to date. You gotta tell me that story some time." He dug his elbow into Jeff's side, grinning widely.

Jeff's feet suddenly forgot to move. Claudia was coming back? He hadn't really expected to see her again. He should have known that she'd graduate eventually, but he'd lost track of the time. He had to admit that he probably was avoiding thinking about it. There's reality for you: *whack*!

"Jeff, wake up. Ha! You didn't know it, did you?" Stewart crowed. "Okay, now you have to come have a beer or two. I want the whole story. Let's go. Move your ass. Get in your van and drive three blocks that way, turn left, go until you see the gas station—"

"Okay, okay, I know the way." Jeff frowned. "I could use a beer too. In fact, now I think I need something stronger than that. You might have to drive me home later, Stewart. Shit."

Stewart led the way in his Camaro. Jeff followed, his mind wandering: Claudia's long slender legs, her thick brown hair, the delicate line of her neck leading down to the soft curve of her breasts. He could hardly stand it. He tucked his van into a space way in back of the parking lot, just in case he had to leave it there all night. Like a doomed man, he allowed Stewart to drag him to a dark booth in the corner.

Stewart waved down a girl with an order pad, and told her to bring a couple shots of tequila and a pitcher of beer. They sat in the gloomy darkness until the drinks came. Stewart handed Jeff a slice of the lime and the salt shaker. Only after they had taken the shots and had their first swallows of beer did Stewart finally lean back with a satisfied sigh. "Now I am happy. And I'm ready to hear the story. You still have a thing for her, right? What'd she do to you, man?"

As the alcohol soaked in, Jeff could feel tension releasing from his shoulders and down through his arms. He took a deep breath. "It was pretty serious. At least, it was for me. I don't really know whether it ever was for her. But she left for college, and that was the end of it."

Stewart looked at him waiting. Jeff stared back, his jaw clenched.

"But what happened? That can't be all there is."

"Well, I'm sorry to disappoint you. That's the whole story."

"But wait. How long did you go out?"

"I don't know." Jeff thought about it for a while. He threw down a handful of peanuts, and raised his beer to his lips again. The first time he had noticed her, when was that? It was at the quarry during the hot summer of their junior year. She was often there swimming laps. She usually stayed apart from the larger crowds of giggling girls and their jock boyfriends, but she had a couple of friends she hung around with.

Finally, one evening, the pool had closed and she was standing outside alone waiting for her ride. "I don't know where my mom is," she'd said. "I thought she knew what time I'd be done here."

So he had offered her a ride home on his motorcycle, and she'd said yes. It was quite a rush, when he placed his helmet on her head and adjusted the strap. She had no fear, that one. In fact, she seemed exhilarated by the whole experience. She held her arms tightly around his waist and shouted directions into his ear so he could hear over the noise of the engine and the wind. He had a hint of things to come, though, when he dropped her off at home and her parents had both come running angrily out of the house to help her off the bike. They hadn't even addressed him. They just watched her give him back his helmet, and then led her, meek and subdued, into the house, leaving him out on the street alone.

They had seen each other many times since then, but he had never taken her home on his motorcycle again. Somehow she always had a reason why he should leave her at the library or at a friend's house.

He shook himself out of his reverie. "We dated…oh…about a year and a half." He waved to the server to bring them two more shots. "Then she got tired of slumming and went off to college." He set up the salt for their second round.

"What a bitch," Stewart looked sympathetic. "And she's been living the classy life since then, huh?"

"I wouldn't know," he spoke grimly. "I haven't heard from her. I didn't even know she was coming home." In fact, Mr. Gilmore, Claudia's father, had led him to believe that Claudia would never be back. Her powerful lawyer father had called Jeff right before she was to leave for college and invited him to his office for a meeting. Jeff had even put on a tie, thinking they were going to have a man-to-man talk about their mutual love for this goddess. Jeff had prepared a speech in which he assured Claudia's father that he planned to work hard and be a good husband to her someday. He never got the chance to make that speech.

Instead, he'd found himself listening to one. Mr. Gilmore ordered Jeff not to contact his daughter ever again. He said that Claudia was from a superior background and that Jeff did not fit in with their family. He was merciless in his assessment of Jeff's chances with her. Though he didn't say it directly, he implied that Claudia had enjoyed his attentions but had no desire to maintain their relationship.

Jeff downed a second shot and watched Stewart swallow his. "Anyway, she didn't want to live as the wife of a construction worker."

"That's rotten! Well, it's her loss. You're better off without her."

Jeff suddenly felt irritated with Stewart. Though he'd been thinking things just like that to himself for almost four years, he didn't want anyone else saying them. "She was an angel, Stewart. Never said an unkind thing in all the time I knew her. She was perfect for me."

"Doesn't sound like it. She wouldn't have just walked away from you like that if she had any real class."

"She didn't really just walk away from me." Jeff spoke slowly, thinking back to the last two weeks before she left for college. "I don't know that she had a choice. Her folks had these plans for her. And then once I figured out what they were and that I didn't fit in with them, I didn't fight it. I think I was waiting for some sort of signal from her that she was willing to cross her parents, but I never got it. They had this power over her. She was a completely different person when they were around."

They were both quiet. Stewart was looking steadily at Jeff now, with a slight smile at the corners of his mouth. He poured them both some more beer. "So. Y' gonna call her? Give her another chance?"

CHAPTER 3

Claudia looked at the other faces around the table. Her father's showed anger, her mother's, resignation. Benjamin was the only one who wasn't showing any emotion at all. He was still methodically taking one bite of his food after another. She couldn't understand the undercurrents of emotions and didn't really want to address them, so she got up from the table and went to the front hallway where her sister, Zoë, had dropped a backpack onto the floor and was pulling loose the laces of her hiking boots.

"Hey, Zoë." Claudia smiled encouragingly.

Zoë jumped, pushed her tangled brown hair from her eyes and turned to look. "Claudia?" She leaped up to fling herself into Claudia's arms. "I'm so glad you're back." Her voice dropped to a furtive whisper. "I have so much to talk to you about."

Claudia knelt to help Zoë with her laces. "We'll have lots of time for that, Zoë. I'm glad to see you again too."

"We're in the middle of dinner here!" Their father's voice boomed from the direction of the dining room.

Zoë wrestled her boots off of her feet. She threw them into the corner of the closet along with her backpack and stalked into the dining room.

Claudia followed her in and took her seat at the table, while her parents berated her younger sister.

"Zoë," began their mother, "you know that we always have dinner at six o'clock."

"I know, Mom. But I'm here, okay?"

"Your mother works hard to put dinner on the table, young lady," their father joined in sternly. "You need to learn to look at the time and plan ahead."

Zoë rolled her eyes and sighed heavily. "Ben, can I have some of that casserole?"

"Zoë," her mother sighed. "What have I told you about cleaning up before you come to the table?"

Zoë shook her hair away from her eyes and looked at the grime on the back of her hands. "First you yell at me for not getting to the table fast enough, then you yell that I didn't stop off at the bathroom on the way. You always manage to find something to criticize me about, don't you?"

Her father's glare got fiercer, but before he could explode, Claudia intervened.

"So. Everyone." The volume of her own voice surprised even herself, and all eyes turned toward her. She had succeeded in shifting the focus away from Zoë but now found herself unsure what to do with it. "I noticed you got some new furniture, Mom," she improvised. "I love the way the living room looks."

Her mother looked at her blankly for a moment, then she laughed. "Oh, darling, I bought that couch several years ago. I almost forgot."

"Well it looks new to me. And what are those paintings on the wall? They seem to be a set, and I don't recognize the artist."

"You don't? But Jeremy Hutchinson is a very up-and-coming young painter. He had a show just last spring in Beaufort's gallery downtown. In fact, I got those pieces there, and I'm thinking of commissioning him to do another one for us. I just haven't thought of the theme yet."

"So," Claudia turned to her father, "are there any good concerts coming to town this summer?"

He wiped the corners of his mouth with his napkin before speaking. "Yes, the board pulled off quite a coup this year. We have the Chicago Symphony coming for the Mozart Festival in August, as well as the Moscow Philharmonic. We expect to draw a larger turnout than ever before. The Burnham Advertising Agency is working on a full-page spread in the Chicago Tribune. They've arranged for tourist buses to bring folks out from as far away as Des Moines, and there are going to be several television spots closer to the time. The hotels are already gearing up for a very busy season."

"That does sound like an accomplishment," Claudia praised. Her father preened visibly. "I'll look forward to the festival."

Claudia's mother finally spoke. "Your father has worked very hard to pull this off." She looked around the table. "I hope the whole family can attend the festival together. It would be such a show of support for all his efforts."

Benjamin looked up from his casserole, "It will depend on my internship, Dad. You know that. I'm not sure yet where I'm going or when I have to be there. You understand."

"Of course, Benjamin, I know I can count on you to try. And of course, your studies come first."

"And Dad," Claudia spoke hesitantly, not wanting to spoil the good mood, "I hope I can come to the festival, but I should have a job by then. I don't know what kind of hours I'll be working."

Zoë had to put her own two cents in. "I might be busy too. I can't predict my whole summer right now."

Claudia's attempt at peacemaking was not going very well. Her father scowled at both girls and said, "There is no good reason why you should not be able to be part of the family for this event. You shouldn't be making plans that interfere with the festival."

"Oh, Dad," Zoë said dismissively. "I don't even like going to the festival. It's just a lot of boring rich people spouting about how much they know about music."

Claudia gasped at Zoë's bluntness and searched for a way to ward off a storm. Before she could say anything, her mother chuckled nervously and said, "Zoë. I'm sure you don't really mean that."

Zoë glared, but before she could level a retort, Claudia stumbled on, "Let's see what happens when the time comes. So, anyway. Tell me some more about what you've been up to."

Everyone's head turned toward Zoë, who immediately became defensive.

"I don't know if now is the time to tell you everything."

Her father looked thunderous. "Answer your sister, young lady!"

"What does it matter to you what I'm up to?" Zoë said indignantly. "You think I'm going to tell Claudia all about myself while you're sitting here just waiting to jump all over me? Forget that! It's none of your business!" She banged on the table with her fist. She stood up, filled her plate, grabbed a roll, and carried the whole thing out of the room, noisily slamming the door behind her.

Claudia was shaken. She looked down at her own plate. She hadn't finished her dinner, but now she had no appetite for it. How could the act of eating bring so much conflict? She tried to remember what meals had been like when she was Zoë's age. Were they the emotional mine fields they seemed to be now?

One thing she did know, she was never as openly contrary as Zoë was to her parents. No, Claudia had never screamed at the dinner table. She was usually quiet, trying not to be noticed.

She stole a look at her brother. Benjamin had always been the family wonder child. So gifted and smart, he had drawn all their parents' attention to himself. Making sure that Benjamin always had the right teachers and the right classes, with his amazing potential, took all their energy. They had done well too. He graduated at the head of his class, and got into all the colleges he applied to. Then, when he graduated from the university summa cum laude, he had his pick of medical schools to go to. Now it seemed he was getting to choose his internship in the same way.

She remembered when she was younger and Benjamin first left for college, feeling suddenly under her parents' microscope. She had tried every way she could think of to please them. She had graduated from high school with a very good grade-point average, but next to Benjamin's stellar record, it looked mediocre. She then went to a good university out east, but ended up getting a degree in a field that held no status and no interest to her parents or their high class friends. She had thought at one time that she would major in pre-law, but it hadn't really interested her. Anthropology had, so she switched. Did that offend her father? She hadn't thought that what she did mattered much to him; he had always been cold to her. For some reason, she felt driven to try to gain his approval. But she had always had limited success.

At one time she thought she might escape the depressing cycle by finding a husband. She thought it should be easy in the university setting; there were so many young men around, all looking for a mate. And yes, she did date some. But none of those dates had ever led anywhere significant. College men were so uninteresting. They all talked about the same boring things while they were out together, and usually wanted the same things from her—first sex, then more sex, then a commitment.

She admitted, sex was fun. But not so fun that it made her want to spend her whole life with any one of those young men. So she had passed them all up, and now she was back at home again.

Suddenly, the others had finished their meal and were beginning to get up from the table. "You can do the dishes, Claudia." Her mother's eyes were on her. Claudia obediently began stacking plates at the table.

Benjamin murmured his excuses and disappeared up the stairs. Claudia's father headed for his den.

She usually enjoyed doing dishes. She knew that here in the kitchen she could perform the simple tasks necessary to achieve a goal. She filled the sink with soapy water so hot she could barely touch it. It was almost therapeutic, to feel the burn as she plunged her arms in up to her elbows. Perspiration began to gather into droplets on her forehead, but it felt good, like a sauna. She closed her eyes and breathed in the steam. It didn't have its usual hypnotic effect on her this time. She just couldn't shake the sadness that she had felt as soon as she got home.

Two hours later, she had brought the last box in from the car. It did turn out to be necessary to store most of her things in the basement, but she managed to put away her summer clothes in the closet where she could get to them and made space for her personal items in the hall bathroom.

Now to get the newspaper and start browsing for jobs. She headed down the stairs toward the front hallway, but as she passed her father's den, she heard her parents' voices.

"Roger, I'm ready to buy those tickets for our trip to Europe. Would you look at these dates with me again? I don't want any conflicts with any of the other activities we've planned."

"Hmmm. Don't forget the festival I want to attend at Versailles this year. I believe those dates are in September."

"Yes, don't worry. I worked that in. If we leave Paris right after the class at the Sorbonne, we'll have four days to visit a few wineries in the Loire Valley before coming back to Versailles. I'm sure it will be enough time."

Claudia thought it odd that they hadn't mentioned their vacation at dinner. If they had plans for the family, she would need to keep those dates free. On the other hand, she hadn't been invited along on any of their other trips these last four years. She just thought that maybe, now that she was home, she might be included. She almost knocked on the door but something stopped her. She continued down the hallway. She found the newspaper and headed back to her room.

She paused at the door to the den again. Their conversation had apparently come to an end, because just as she was passing the door, it opened and her mother stood on the other side.

"Hello, dear, we were just talking about our summer vacation," her mother said, motioning to Claudia to enter.

"Yes," her father said. "We will be in Europe several weeks at the end of the summer. Now that you're home, you'll be able to keep an eye on Zoë while we're gone so the house doesn't fall down around her head." Both of her parents chuckled at his wit.

Well, that answered that. "You mean, you're going to Europe alone." The newspaper in her shaking hand rustled.

Her father looked up surprised. "Well, of course. Who else would we go with?"

Her mother put her hand on her husband's shoulder and looked up at him adoringly. "Yes, darling. This is our time together, after all."

Claudia stood with her mouth open, "But…"

Her father interrupted. "And now I need to get back to my work."

CHAPTER 4

Claudia spent a restless night with a pad of paper by her bed. Every now and then she turned on the light and wrote herself another reminder note. *Take car to mechanic. Rewrite resume. Call Andi.* Finally she ran out of things to worry about and fell asleep. In the morning, she sat down to breakfast and watched her family rush around the house getting ready for their day.

"Claudia, could you finish up these dishes? I'm due at Eileen's in twenty minutes for my perm." Her mother turned to straighten her husband's tie and give him a peck on the cheek.

"Goodbye, Claudia," her father said. "Don't forget to call my mechanic. I've left the number by the telephone in the hall." He reached for his briefcase and headed for the door.

"Thanks, Dad," Claudia replied. "It's on my list. I'm planning to go into town and start my job search."

"Good girl."

Benjamin appeared briefly at the kitchen door. "Mom, I won't be home for dinner. I have a study group meeting at campus. We're going to just grab sandwiches at Subway."

"Benjamin. That's not a healthy dinner. Claudia, please wake Zoë up before you go. I don't want her to be late for school. She only has a few weeks left to go, and she has to be on her toes the entire time if she's going to get a passing grade."

Benjamin and their father left together, calling their good-byes. Their mother finally gathered her jacket and her purse and vanished.

Claudia immediately went to knock on Zoë's door. She waited until she heard a grunt and then went back to her chores.

When she had cleaned up the kitchen and made her phone calls, she headed upstairs to get ready for her job search. Dressed in a crisp blouse and skirt, she studied herself in the full length mirror on her closet door. It was difficult to look at herself without seeing all her faults at once, especially now that she was back in her family home. Hearing her mother's voice in her head, she stood straight and pulled in her stomach. She brushed a little mascara onto her lashes to accent her eyes (too pale, too close together), drew an outline around her lips (too thin), and filled them in with a peach color to match her scarf.

Smoothing her skirt down over her slender hips, she sighed. The skirt would surely be wrinkled by the time she had her first interview. Her knees were rather knobby, and her nose was too large, but it was the best she could do.

Walking through the front hallway, she remembered to retrieve her thoroughly marked-up newspaper, and left the house. She was wearing sensible shoes so she could drop her car at the mechanic's and visit various businesses in town on foot. She had carefully mapped her route so she would end up at Josie's Grill for lunch. Her friend Andi would be meeting her there, so they could catch up on each other's news and make plans for their summer.

✳ ✳ ✳

After a long morning of trudging down Carlsburg's sidewalks, peering at addresses, waiting in office entryways, perching on uncomfortable wooden chairs, and trying to balance applications on magazines held on her knees, Claudia was ready for a break. She walked the two blocks to the Grill and went inside. Looking around, she didn't see anyone she recognized, so she gave the hostess her name and sat on a bench to wait for an open booth.

She was looking forward to seeing Andi again. Andi was one of those real friends who would always be there when you needed her, and would always tell the truth as she saw it. She was a genuine person—always the same no matter who she was with. Someone she knew once called such a person a "pure flame," because nothing could make her alter her course. Most of us, Claudia mused, especially Claudia herself, were too sensitive to what others thought not to change just a little when someone else was around. The best she could do was to choose her friends by who she became when she was with them.

With Andi, Claudia became someone she liked a lot. She felt free and easy with Andi. She could relax. They had fun together, and Andi made Claudia laugh. Andi even laughed when Claudia made a crack. She felt sharp and witty when they were together. But when she wasn't up to being witty, she knew that was okay too. If she was tired and her shoulders slumped a little, Andi didn't notice, or if she did, she was more likely to rub them a little, knowing that's what Claudia needed.

Right now, what Claudia really needed was a good foot rub, but she knew that wasn't probably going to happen, so when Andi walked through the door of the restaurant, she painfully rose and let the hostess lead them to their seats at a booth in a quiet corner of the dining room.

"There's one more person coming," Andi told the hostess. "She'll ask for Andi, so that's me, okay?"

Andi saw the query in Claudia's eyes, and said, "I ran into Naomi this morning and told her to join us. Did you know she was back too?"

"Naomi?" Claudia smiled, "How wonderful! I'm glad you did that!"

Andi slid back off the bench, "I didn't hug you yet, Claudia. Welcome back! I'm so glad to see you!"

Claudia got up, they exchanged hugs, kissed each other's cheeks and sat back down. She was surprised to notice that her eyes were a little damp. Wiping them, she said, "I'm sorry. I must be tired from walking around all morning looking for a job."

"That's not all it is though, is it?" A knowing look was on Andi's face. "How's the family?"

"I swear, you're a mind reader! It's been such a long time since I've been here. Everything's changed. My mom's gotten all new furniture in the living room. Zoë's growing up and angry all the time. Benjamin is as quiet as ever, always the studious one. I never know what he's thinking." She thought a moment. "Yes, a lot has changed, but a lot has stayed the same."

Andi nodded. "Yes, that's what I thought."

They were interrupted by the arrival of their friend Naomi. Amid the shrieks of greetings and more hugs and kisses, it finally seemed to Claudia that she was home.

In many ways, Naomi and Andi were polar opposites. Whereas Andi kept her straight brown hair pulled back into a neat but simple ponytail, Naomi spent probably an hour and a half every morning straightening and then curling her silky blonde hair into a gorgeous up-do. Andi cut her nails as short as possible and then left them alone. She only cut them again when they got so long they started tearing on things. Naomi's slender, delicate fingers were capped by perfect but completely natural nails, filed to a lovely oval and painted carefully to match whatever she was wearing that day. Today she was wearing a pastel pink linen suit, complete with jacket and matching flats. Claudia marveled that Naomi managed to look fresh and classy in that color; Claudia knew that she would feel silly in it herself. Claudia unconsciously leaned toward colors that would help her blend in: browns, grays, sometimes black. Andi wore denim cargo pants today, as she did most days. With her job at the lumber yard, it was the most practical and comfortable attire, which was a good thing, because that's what she wanted to wear anyway. Claudia and Andi sometimes ribbed Naomi, in a good-natured manner, that on her wedding day, she wouldn't have to do anything different—just throw on a white dress and walk down the aisle. Naomi took it all in stride.

As different as the three friends were, they'd been close since junior high, where they first became acquainted in Mr. Howard's biology class. Dissecting the fetal pig together was the activity that cemented their relationship into a pattern that would repeat itself over and over throughout the years. Andi had been the fearless one who cut the pig open, while Naomi took perfect notes, once she got over her fear of looking inside the animal's skin. Claudia had insisted that they meet after school hours, so they could coach each other on the different muscles and organs. They rehearsed it so well that they got top grades on their lab workbook and aced the exam at the end of the quarter.

The three quickly looked at their menus and made their orders, so they could get on with their talking. Though they had written to each other frequently while Claudia and Naomi were away at college, they hadn't been together in all that time. It was as though no time had gone by at all.

Claudia took a sip of her water. "Naomi, when did you get back? Are you really completely done with school? What are you going to do next?"

Naomi smiled. "Okay, I'll go first. But then you have to tell me everything you're up to." She opened up her napkin to place it neatly on her lap. "I've been back for two weeks."

Andi interrupted, "Yeah, I saw you in Walgreen's the other day. You were equipping your new bathroom, right?"

"Yes, I got one of the apartments in the new building over on the corner of Wright and Seventh Street."

"That was fast!" Claudia was impressed.

"Well, I got a job at an actuarial firm in town and I wanted to live nearby. Besides, my folks have three foster children now, and my room is taken up."

"Didn't that make you a little sad? That they didn't even save your room?" Claudia knew how hurt she felt coming home to her mother's clothing in her closet.

"Oh no, I really needed the push to get out and into my own place. Besides, the kids are sweet. I get to be the visiting big sister now. They're so excited when I come over. We play cards together and bake cookies."

Claudia shook her head in wonder. She couldn't even imagine playing cards with her sister and brother. "I really hope one of these jobs comes through. I need to get out of my house too."

"Where have you been applying?" Andi asked. "I could probably get you a job in the office at the lumber yard."

Claudia looked at her friend in dismay. Another desk job. "I'm having terrible luck finding something relevant to my major. My advisor told me that I'd have a hard time getting work with just a bachelor's in anthropology. I knew it too. But I love learning about different cultures and studying the evidence for the ones that are gone." She shook her head sadly. "But how to turn that into an asset, and how to do that here in Carlsburg, I just don't know."

Naomi looked at Claudia sympathetically. "So why don't you go on to grad school?"

"My parents told me it was time to stop wasting money just fooling around and come home and get a job." Claudia said. "I'm pretty certain I could have gotten an assistantship but they wouldn't let me even talk about it. I swear, I felt like an adult for four years, and now that I'm home, I'm back to feeling like an idiot child again. How does a thing like this happen?"

Andi showed her indignation. "Claudia, you are an adult! Why do you let them control you like this?"

"I don't really know!" Claudia shook her head in disbelief. "It happens and I don't seem to have a way to break the pattern. I'm not like that usually. I like to think of myself as someone who is pretty self-confident."

Naomi broke in and tried to get the conversation back on safer ground. "So, what kind of job are you looking for?"

"My father said that I should fit into any job that called for working with people. It made some sense so that's what I've focused on. I found a company that advertised for a sales representative, another one that needs someone to plan conventions, and then there's a job posted at the Gazette. I'd be writing human interest stories. That one actually seems interesting."

At that moment, the waitress set a plate of bread on the table, and Andi began slathering butter on a nice thick slice. "I'm starving."

Naomi delicately sipped her water, pretending not to see the bread. She held onto her willowy shape with an iron will, which Claudia admired tremendously but couldn't emulate very well, as hard as she tried. Andi didn't seem to try at all. She had always been a girl with an appetite, but she also seemed to use it up. She was strong and muscular and didn't shirk physical labor. She wasn't fat by any means, but you wouldn't call her willowy either.

Finally giving in to the sight of Andi chewing on the heavily seeded bread, Claudia took a slice for herself too. She buttered it well and then tried to eat it slowly to make up for her lack of willpower. "I've got about five more ads to answer this afternoon, and then I'll quit for the day."

Andi swallowed happily and licked her lips. "I sure wish you'd come to work with me. It would be so much fun having you there."

Unlike her two friends, Andi hadn't gone to college, though she was bright enough. Her grades hadn't been consistently high throughout high school, and her parents, being simple working people without a lot of extra money to spend, didn't push it. Claudia watched her friend and wondered, *Could I be happy living that life? It seems so much less complicated than my own.*

"How do you like it there, Andi? What do you do all day long?" Claudia asked.

"Every day is different, and I've been there long enough that I've done just about every job they have." Andi reached for another slice of bread. "My favorite is when people come in with fun projects in mind and I get to help them choose wood and materials for their cabinets or tools for their homes." She grinned broadly. "I love being the expert."

"I can't imagine myself becoming an expert on woodworking, Andi," Claudia laughed. "We're going to have to settle for seeing each other during our off-hours."

Andi raised her eyebrows playfully. "I also like seeing the hunky young construction guys come in for parts. I get to help them work out some really big orders sometimes." She nodded out the window and waved.

Claudia turned just in time to see a large white van pulling out of a parking spot across the street. She froze when she saw who was in the driver's seat waving back.

Jeff Gordon's eyes met Claudia's for a brief instant. His tires squealed and he drove away. She watched the back of his van disappear around the corner.

Naomi touched Claudia's hand. "Claudia, are you okay? That was Jeff, wasn't it? It's been a long time since you two dated. You don't have feelings for him any more do you?"

"I guess I do still feel something," Claudia said shakily, "for some reason."

"Well, he's really sweet." Andi said. "And he's one of the best electricians in town now. All the contractors ask for him. I see him come in a lot."

Claudia said wistfully, "I bet he is sweet. I always thought so."

"Why did you break up with him?" Naomi asked her.

"I don't think I did." She was still confused. "I was getting ready to go to college, and I was really hoping we could stay in touch and see each other during my breaks, but then suddenly, he stopped calling me. And then I left. I haven't heard or spoken with him since."

Their food came. Naomi drizzled some dressing over her salad. "Claudia, why didn't you ever come back for a visit?"

"I actually did come, but not often, and not for long. My parents paid for me to fly home a couple of times for holidays, but then I felt obliged to spend all my time with them doing what they wanted me to do. I would fly away so quickly again that I never had time to call my friends. I'm so sorry about that."

"Your folks are really strange people." Andi lifted a slice of pizza from the plate, and took a big bite of the cheese that was hanging off the side. "Oh my god, that is so good!" She swallowed, drank some of her Coke, and went on, "They were always nice enough to me, but I didn't feel like they really liked having me around. You know, sometimes you can chat with your friends' moms, but your mom didn't ever seem like she wanted to."

Claudia knew exactly what she meant. Neither of her parents had ever expressed much interest in Claudia's activities or ideas, much less those of her friends. It was even hard just to find something to talk about at the dinner table. But she was going to have to get along anyway. "I know what you're saying, Andi. My parents have a different style. Not very nurturing."

"Now your sister, Zoë," Andi went on. "She's a real person. I really like that kid. But I'd worry about her if I were you."

Claudia furrowed her brow. "What do you mean?"

"Well, I've seen her around town with some guys that I wouldn't trust as far as I could throw." She sprinkled some red pepper flakes on her pizza. "She looked much too interested in what they have to sell, if you know what I mean."

"No, I don't know what you mean." Claudia narrowed her eyes. "What are they selling?" She stared at Andi, waiting. "You don't mean drugs, do you? My mom told me she was worried about that."

Andi nodded.

Naomi put her own fork down. "Claudia, you should talk to your sister. She's going to get herself into a lot of trouble—if she isn't already."

"Oh dear." Claudia had never had to deal with anything like this. Even though she had been on her own while she was at school, she had purposely associated only with people like herself, quiet and studious. She had made friends, even with some who might be considered a lot more fun-loving and into parties than she was, but she rarely participated herself. Besides, she had little interest in people like that, so she basically ignored that side of life. Now she was going to have to address it. Zoë was getting mixed up in things she shouldn't. It was time for Claudia to learn to be a good sister.

CHAPTER 5

Saturday morning, Claudia slept in while the rest of the family scurried off, busy as usual. At ten, Zoë's tousled head appeared at the landing of the staircase. "I was supposed to be up two hours ago! Mom and Dad are going to kill me. I just missed the Saturday morning class they signed me up for." She skipped down the stairs and threw herself onto the sofa beside Claudia. "Oh well, I didn't want to go anyway. What are you reading?"

Claudia stuck her bookmark into her book and handed it over. "It's just a mystery. I felt like doing something mindless for a while. What's this class you were supposed to go to?"

"My grades haven't been that great, so Mom is sending me off to learn better study skills." Zoë rolled her eyes and chewed at one of her fingernails. "I don't need to learn to study. I just need to be done with this boring school, so I can get out and do something more interesting."

"Do you have something in mind?" Claudia smiled. She remembered feeling this way at that age. School had seemed horribly dull when she compared it with all the wonderful lives that she imagined other people living.

"You'll think it's stupid."

"I think you'd be surprised. I've had my own dreams too, you know." Claudia reached out to pat Zoë on the arm. "I used to imagine traveling the world, being a great explorer, studying other cultures. I wanted to learn lots of languages and do exotic things, like carrying water for three miles so I could cook dinner over a wood fire."

"I bet that's why you ended up studying anthropology, isn't it?"

"Yes, but I had other dreams too. I thought it would be exciting to be a brilliant artist, living in a garret creating beautiful paintings that people would clamor to possess."

"Yes, I imagine the same thing about myself! But I didn't know you were a dreamer. I thought you always just did your thing like you knew exactly where you were going."

"I don't always tell people what I'm thinking. But yes, sometimes I wish I could be somewhere else."

"Well, I have all sorts of ideas about what to do when I'm free of this place."

"Tell me more about your dreams, Zoë."

"I don't know."

"Come on. I told you mine."

"Okay. I want to be a bus driver."

"No you don't."

"I knew you would laugh at me."

"I'm not laughing, I just don't believe you. Are you looking for the thing that is going to irritate Dad the most?"

Zoë laughed. "That's partly true, you're right. But I might actually enjoy it. I would get to joke with people all day long, and there wouldn't be any bosses standing over me watching and criticizing."

"True. Have you ever thought, though, about what you would want to do if you didn't have Mom and Dad to push against?"

"I can't even imagine not having them to fight with. They've been on my case since the beginning of time. The first thing I want is to go far away where they can't reach me."

Claudia's smile faded. There was a time when she felt that way too. She had thought that if she could just be patient, and finish her degree, she'd be able to finally go into the wonderful world and do exciting things with her life. Yet, here she was, trapped at home. She didn't want to discourage Zoë by telling her that all the work and goals just lead you back to the same old thing. But that's how it had been for her lately.

"Maybe if you were just a little more patient, Zoë," Claudia began.

Zoë rolled her eyes. "That's how adults talk." She punched her pillow and stuffed it behind her back on the couch. "Sometimes you have to take matters into your own hands."

Claudia couldn't help but admire her gutsy younger sister, though hearing her talk this way alarmed her. Her cautious side won out. "It's always a good thing to think about where your life is going in the long run, but—"

"I'm tired of waiting for the long run," Zoë declared. "Anyway, I don't want to talk about that."

Claudia was wondering how she could bring up the subject that Andi had touched on the other day. "Zoë ..." She hesitated.

"Hmmm?"

"Tell me about your life."

Zoë raised her eyebrows, "Why? What do you want to know?"

"I don't know. You don't like school. What are you doing these days? Who are your friends? What are they like?"

"They're okay. We just hang out mostly. Walk around town. Whatever." Zoë picked up a magazine and started leafing through it.

Claudia opened up her book again. They sat there together in silence for a while until Zoë said, "You know, I really just like being alone a lot of the time. Nobody to tell me I'm doing something wrong, or not doing something I'm supposed to be doing."

Claudia smiled sympathetically, "Nobody to pressure you to be someone you're not."

Tears sprang into Zoë's eyes. "Exactly!" She tossed the magazine back on the table. "Do you know where I was the happiest?"

"Tell me."

"Do you remember your last summer before college, you and your friends took your tents and sleeping bags to the forest preserve for a weekend, and you let me come with? I got to have my own tent and sit by the fire and eat what I wanted all weekend and nobody bothered with me all day. I know you guys just thought I was a little kid tagging along, but I felt really grown up and independent the whole time, and nobody nagged me." She sighed blissfully. "It was wonderful! Sometimes, I just want to go and live there, and pretend the outside world doesn't exist!"

Claudia thought back on that time. That was right in the middle of the brief time when she and Jeff were the most in love. They had gone to the woods with several other friends, both boys and girls. Claudia had invited Zoë so their parents wouldn't get suspicious and question them too closely about who else was going to be there. Then, once they got to the site, Claudia and Jeff spent most of the three days and two nights walking through the woods together or sitting by the campfire cuddling and gazing into each other's eyes. Luckily Zoë actually did turn out to be capable of taking care of herself, because Claudia wasn't paying any attention to her at all.

"Wow, Zoë." Claudia closed her book again and placed it on the coffee table. "I forgot all about that camping trip of ours. My experience of it was a little different of course." She smiled slyly.

"Yes, I think you and Jeff barely knew what was going on around you."

"Shh! I can't imagine what Mom and Dad would think if they knew what we were doing that weekend and who I was with, even though it happened so long ago."

"You're right," Zoë agreed. "I think they'd have a fit."

The sound of a door slamming upstairs interrupted them. Zoë jumped up and said, "Time for me to go hide again!"

Claudia opened her book and tried to look like she was engrossed in it just as Benjamin entered.

"I thought I heard voices down here," he said looking around.

Claudia smiled. "Zoë and I were talking. I think she was afraid it was Mom or Dad coming to scold her for something."

Benjamin grinned too as he threw himself into an easy chair. "They really are on her case a lot."

"I'm surprised you noticed. You don't always seem very involved."

"Well, I do have a pretty full schedule just keeping up with my classes at the university."

Claudia felt abashed. "I'm sorry, you're right."

Benjamin lowered his voice to a conspiratorial tone. "It also makes for a good excuse when I want to stay out of their fights."

"Ah." She should definitely sit on the couch more often. "So, are you really studying in your room all the time?"

"A lot of the time I am. But not always."

Claudia waited for a while, but nothing more was coming. "Benjamin, do you like what you're doing?"

Benjamin looked thoughtful, "I wonder that myself. I guess I'm meant to do what I'm doing. But sometimes I wonder where I would be without Mom and Dad opening so many doors for me. What would I do if I had to open them myself? I'm not so sure."

"Dad is really proud of you."

"I know. That makes it that much harder for me to think straight sometimes. What if I decided I didn't really want to be a doctor?"

"Whoa. Do you mean it? Is that really how you feel?"

"Well sometimes, I think I might just like to be a small town G.P. instead of a big city cardiologist, like Dad seems to have his heart set on. I'd like to really get to know my patients, and take care of all their families, not just one part of them."

"Have you tried to tell Dad this?"

"Of course not. Can you imagine what he'd say? No, I don't think I can handle that kind of conflict. Maybe I'll like cardiology. It *is* really interesting." He sounded almost convinced.

"But ..." Claudia couldn't just leave it at that. "You of all people..."

"What?" Benjamin smiled. "What do you mean by that?"

"I mean...I mean, if even you don't get to direct your own life..."

Just then the telephone rang. Claudia's pleading eyes followed Benjamin as he got up to answer it. She looked at her book again but couldn't pick it up for all the thoughts swirling around in her head. She was surprised when Benjamin dropped the phone in her lap and quickly left the room.

"Hello?" she spoke hesitantly into the phone.

A man's voice came over the line. "Claudia?" She knew that voice. It had spoken words of love to her, many times, whispering into her ear, or over the phone line, softly, insistently, and then never again.

"Jeff."

"I heard you were home."

"Yes."

"How are you?"

"I'm fine. You?"

"I'm fine. Umm. I'd like to see you, Claudia."

"Yes, that would be nice."

"Are you free some time? We could have dinner together."

Claudia's heart was pounding in her ears so she could barely hear him. Tears were welling up in her eyes, but she struggled not to let her emotions show. "Yes, I think I would like that."

"How's Tuesday? I could pick you up at 6:30."

"That would be fine."

"Okay then. I'll see you on Tuesday."

"Yes. Good bye."

Claudia placed the telephone carefully down on the cradle, and then was surprised to find her hand was shaking. She hadn't known those feelings were still so strong, but they felt as fresh as if the hurt had just happened yesterday.

* * *

Jeff hung up the phone and sat staring at it for a full two minutes. He didn't know if he had done the right thing. He had no idea what Claudia's life was like now. She might not even be unattached. She'd had a lot of time to find someone else since they'd last seen each other. But, as Stewart had made him remember, there had been a lot between them at one time. And he had given up much too easily. It was time to remedy that.

CHAPTER 6

Claudia raced down the sidewalk in the pouring rain with only a newspaper to hold over her head. She was drenched. She ducked under an awning just outside a bank. She found herself in the midst of a small group of unrelated strangers, standing and chatting as though they had just gathered around the water cooler and would be on their way when their break was over.

Peering around the corner, she saw that the sky to the west was full of dark and menacing clouds, moving fast. What she wouldn't give to have her car back from the mechanic, but he had told her that it was going to take a few more days to get the part that was needed. She looked up and down the street for a bus stop, but the rain was a solid sheet of water now, and visibility was almost nonexistent. She settled into the back corner of the doorway and sat down on the step to go over the tattered, and now soaked, classified section one more time.

She'd been out pounding the pavement so much that the newspaper she was holding in her hand had marks on almost half of the job notices. At first she had tried to apply just for the jobs that seemed interesting to her, but now she was stopping in at all the other businesses in town. Nothing had come through, even though she'd had several interviews that she had felt good about. It seemed to her that once she mentioned the degree she had just completed, the interviewer lost interest and the questions became perfunctory. She was getting frantic. Anything would do at this point, as long as she could start earning some money and get her own place.

Somebody new joined the crowd, and everyone in his turn adjusted his position to accommodate the addition to their numbers. Claudia squeezed herself further into the corner without looking up.

"Claudia?" There was a tap on her shoulder. "Is that you?"

She recognized Anthony Emerson, one of the partners at her father's law firm. Instinctively, she reached her hand up to check her hair, and found it desperately in need of combing. Oh well, nothing to be done about that now.

"Good afternoon, Mr. Emerson." She smiled ruefully. "I'm afraid you haven't caught me at my best."

"I think the same could be said for the both of us, my dear." Mr. Emerson said indulgently. "Your father told me that you were back from college and looking for a job."

"Yes sir." She nodded at the newspaper in her hand. "I haven't had a great deal of luck so far, but I'm sure learning my way around town."

He cleared his throat. "Well, I told your father, but maybe he hasn't had a chance to talk to you yet about the opening we have in our secretarial pool. We have a lot of work these days. We could use you on the team."

Claudia pushed her wet hair from in front of her eyes. "Yes, he said that I should apply at the firm. But sir, to work in my father's office?"

He laughed at the distraught look on her face. "Don't worry. We would assign you to someone else, but yes, you'd be in the same office, and could probably drive in together most days."

"Oh dear. I don't know."

"Well, think about it." He pulled out a business card and scribbled a name on the back. "Here's who to ask for when you call. I'll talk to her about you, so she knows I've offered you the job."

She took the card and tucked it safely in her bag. "Thank you, Mr. Emerson. I really appreciate it. If you don't mind though," she smiled and tugged at a sodden lock of her hair, "I think I'll wait until tomorrow, and I can get a fresh start before I drop by."

He chuckled genially. "Of course, dear. I don't think anyone would blame you." At that, he opened his umbrella again and strode away.

Claudia looked after him thoughtfully. It seemed like her father was maneuvering everything around her to meet his own goals. She wondered what those goals were.

✳ ✳ ✳

Home again, Claudia hurried to get out of her wet clothes and into a nice hot bath. Digging through the bathroom cabinet, she found some lavender bath beads, which she poured generously into the bathtub. As the water ran, the fragrant steam filled the room. Finally, she stepped into the tub and lowered herself slowly into the hot water. She took a deep breath and let it out slowly, relaxing for the first time that day. It was surprising how knotted her muscles had become and how nice the heat felt on them now. She leaned back and closed her eyes.

She took her time soaping the cloth. She wanted to be fresh and rested by the time Jeff came to pick her up for dinner. They hadn't seen each other in such a long time, she didn't want anything to mar the occasion. She wondered whether he was thinking similar thoughts as he got ready for their first date in four years. Hmmph. Probably not. He had always been so confident and natural. He wouldn't stew or worry about what impression he was going to make on her. That was probably what had attracted her to him in the first place.

"Claudia." Zoë's voice came through the door. "Mom says that she wants you downstairs."

"Tell her I'm in the bath. I'll be down soon."

As she listened to Zoë's footsteps recede, she sighed and pulled the drain on the tub. Toweling herself dry, she gazed into her reflection in the mirror, took a deep breath, and steeled herself for the scene she expected when her mother learned she'd be having dinner with Jeff tonight. She could still remember her parents' reaction when they first realized that she was involved with a boy who rode a motorcycle.

"Claudia, you should not be seeing a wild boy like that," her mother had sighed, as though repeating a lesson she had told her wayward daughter all her life. "I'm sure he told you some line about how pretty you are, but remember, boys like that always lie to get what they want, and they are always up to no good."

Claudia noticed wryly the implication that if Jeff had called her pretty, it must be a lie. "But Mom, he really is nice," Claudia tried to protest. "And besides, he only gave me a ride home. It was perfectly innocent."

Then her father couldn't resist sneering. "Hah. There is nothing innocent about that boy—or any boy."

"Darling, we don't want to forbid you to see him again, but do keep in mind that we have other goals for you, and they do not include you getting attached to a hometown boy with no future like that one."

Claudia had thought it premature to be talking about her getting attached to this boy who had only given her a ride home once on his motorcycle, but she hadn't argued. She didn't even know if they would see each other again, though she hoped that they would. But she decided she would be careful not to share whatever did happen with her parents.

As it turned out, she and Jeff had been together quite a few more times and their friendship had deepened over the next year and a half into something she felt very strongly. She'd thought he had felt the same, but four years of silence had dashed those hopes. She had spent the years trying to get over the disappointment, but hadn't quite succeeded. Now she was going to have a chance to discover where they stood, and she didn't want her parents' attitudes to affect her own emotions before she could even figure out what they were.

She found her mother sitting in the living room reading a magazine and drinking a glass of iced tea.

"There you are, Claudia. I was thinking that we should cook on the grill tonight. I'm just not in the mood to mess up the kitchen."

"Well actually, Mom, I'll be eating out tonight."

"That's a surprise." Her mother raised her well-shaped eyebrows. "Anybody I know?"

"Well, he's an old friend. You didn't know him well."

"Who is it?"

"Jeff Gordon."

"Hmmph!" Her mother pursed her lips. "Claudia, your father will be disappointed in you. He thought you were over him."

"Mom, he's just a friend. We're going to go out and catch up on things. We haven't seen each other in a long time. There's nothing wrong with that."

"Your father will not approve. He has much higher hopes for you, I know."

Claudia raised her brow. "And what hopes are those, Mom? I'm a little confused about what the two of you actually expect of me."

"Darling," her mother began. "Of course we want you to be happy. He thinks that it's time for you to settle down with an ambitious young man who can make us proud." She sneered. "Jeff Gordon is just a construction worker. He'll never amount to anything."

"Mom, please, I'm just going out to dinner. Don't make a big issue of it. I have to get ready to go. Can we have this conversation another time?"

Claudia turned and headed back up the stairs. Her mother made as though to get up and follow her, but then slapped her magazine in her hand and turned the other way. In her room again, Claudia's heart was pounding and her hand was shaking as she tried to apply her mascara. Finally she blotted away the marks she had made on her cheeks. That would have to do. Why, oh why, couldn't they just be happy for her? Or failing that, leave her alone? They had for most of the last four years. What was going on that they couldn't now?

She heard a light tap, and then Zoë poked her head around the door. Claudia, startled, glanced quickly at the clock.

"No, he's not here yet." Zoë slipped inside and closed the door. "Tell me about Jeff, Claudia." She sat on the end of the bed and leaned forward to whisper. "Why did you like him so much?"

Claudia opened her jar of powder, and began to pat at it with the brush. "Oh Zoë, he was like no one else I'd ever known." She lightly applied the powder to her cheeks and forehead. "You know, as much as Mom and Dad hated it, I think what first appealed to me was that motorcycle." She smiled. "There's just something very powerful and sexy about riding behind a strong man on a motorcycle."

"Oooh, I can just imagine! But that wasn't all, was it?"

"No, of course not." Claudia closed the powder and reached for her blusher. "That would be pretty shallow of me if I only cared about what kind of vehicle he drove, wouldn't it?" She darkened the hollows under her cheekbones, and then sat back to view the results.

"But still, it's pretty important, isn't it?" Zoë teased her laughingly.

"Well, sure!" Claudia picked up her hairbrush and slowly ran it through her thick wavy hair. "But seriously, once I got to know him better, I realized there was so much more to him than that."

"Tell me."

"He was confident but not in a swaggering sort of way, even back then, when we were still only teenagers. He always took charge when we were together. I could never predict what his plans for our dates would be, but they were always so much fun."

She stopped brushing and examined herself in the mirror. "It's really interesting. I'm so passive when I'm with our family, it's like I have no opinions or personality of my own. When I'm with my friends, Andi and Naomi, and with my friends at college, I'm a real person. I make decisions, I can discuss interesting things. People listen to me! I even make people laugh—in a good way! When I was with Jeff, it's almost like I thought he was Dad, and suddenly I was afraid to voice my own thoughts. And yet, he was so nice. I didn't really think he would be like Dad and judge me harshly. But I still couldn't relax and just be me. I'm curious what we'll be like together now."

They both looked up at the sound of a car driving up to the house. Claudia quickly closed up her makeup case and stuck her brush in the drawer. She hugged her sister. "See you later."

Jeff was standing just inside the front door. Though Claudia's mother was usually a perfect hostess, she was standing silently next to him, arms crossed, watching Claudia come down the stairs.

"I hope you won't be home too late. Your father will not be able to sleep until the house is quiet."

"Don't worry, Mrs. Gilmore. I won't keep her out late."

The door closed behind them as they walked down the front steps.

CHAPTER 7

Claudia was even more beautiful than he remembered. Seeing her lovely chestnut hair framing her face, bouncing slightly while she walked as though it had a mind of its own, he forgot himself. Her mother sure seemed hostile. She had probably never expected to hear from him again. Well, too bad for her. It was time to get the parents out of the picture and let the two of them decide for themselves where their relationship was going to go.

She smiled as she approached Jeff's gray Toyota Celica.

"I think I've seen this car before, haven't I?"

"You have. It was my dad's car, back in those days. He handed it down to me, and I've managed to keep it going."

"Do you still have the motorcycle?"

"Of course I do. We can go for a ride some time, if you're interested."

"I'd love that."

They were several blocks away from the house before either of them spoke again.

"It's good to see you again, Jeff."

"I think your mother wasn't happy that I showed up again."

"No, you're right. I don't really understand what my parents have against you." Claudia looked out the window in consternation.

"Your mom must have known about your father's talk with me that last summer and figured I wouldn't be back."

"My father's talk?" Claudia asked hesitantly. "I think I must have missed something."

He looked up surprised. "You don't remember, then?"

"Remember what? I don't think I ever knew! I think we have a lot of talking to do, Jeff."

"It seems we do," Jeff said, but at that moment, they arrived at the restaurant. The hostess led them through the dimly lit dining room to a table for two in a quiet corner.

Jeff watched Claudia's face as she opened up her menu. She was lovely. Gentle Claudia. She always had deferred to his judgment, making him feel strong and masterful. He wondered now, though, whether his pride at showing her what he was capable of had kept her from finding her own strength. This time around, he was determined to give her space. He wanted her to have the same opportunities he had had all his life to make his own choices and discover what his tastes were. It would be hard to hold back, but it would also be exciting, finding out who Claudia really was deep inside. He wondered if she even knew.

Claudia looked up and smiled shyly. "What? Why are you looking at me that way?"

"I just really like looking at you," he replied. "Ignore me. Take your time reading the menu."

"Everything looks so good," she said, poring over the pages in front of her. "What do you like?"

"It's all good. You'd be happy with anything here," he said unhelpfully.

Claudia took a deep breath and studied the menu carefully. Finally she said, "Okay, I'm ready."

Jeff signaled to the waiter who was hovering nearby. They both waited patiently for Claudia, who pointed out the pork chop that she wanted along with a side salad. Jeff ordered the prime rib, and the waiter disappeared. Almost immediately another server came to take away some of their silverware and replace it with other pieces. Instead of the white cloth napkin that was sitting at her place, Claudia was presented with a black one, to match the slacks she was wearing. Claudia's eyes were wide with amazement at the attention they were receiving.

"I see you've become very worldly in my absence," she finally said, keeping a light tone.

Jeff grinned back. "Of course, I had to do something while I waited for you to come back."

Claudia flushed. "But, you didn't know whether I'd be back. I didn't even know."

"You're right. I didn't know. I was just hoping all that time. So, do you want to hear the rest of the story about what your father said to me?"

"It's probably going to make me mad, but I think I should."

"Well, he called me over to his office one day. Early August, I think." He swallowed some of his water. "He never even asked me what my intentions were, just told me I better not have any."

Claudia gasped, but before she could say anything, he went on. "He told me that I wasn't in your social class. He said I would just drag you down. He said you shouldn't be *obliged* to stay in touch with me. I should back off right away, so there would be no pressure on you." Jeff expressed the bitterness he had been feeling ever since that day.

"And you believed him?"

"I didn't know what to believe. He's a very persuasive man, your father. I really felt out of my league just talking to him."

"I had no idea," she spoke in almost a whisper.

"I figured that if he was wrong, or lying to me, you would write me no matter what he said. And then we'd eventually be together."

"And I never did." She shook her head. "I swear, I never ever said such a thing to either of my parents. I never knew what my father had done, or what he was even thinking. About that same time my mom told me she'd seen you out with someone else, and that she heard that you weren't really serious about either me or the other girl. They both kept telling me how wrong you were for me. And then I didn't hear from you again, and I figured they must be right."

The food had arrived. Jeff had wanted Claudia to be impressed by the delicious food there, but she didn't seem able to even put it in her mouth now. Finally she put the fork back down and looked up into Jeff's eyes.

"I can't eat," she said in despair.

"I'm sorry. Maybe I should have waited until after dinner."

"Maybe," Claudia said sadly, looking at her plate. "But I needed to know. You see, when you stopped showing up at our usual spot, I didn't know what to think. And then my mother told me that she heard that you were seeing someone else, even before I left."

"I don't know what she was talking about. You were the only one I ever wanted. I couldn't look at anyone else. I didn't date at all for months after you left. Even then, it was only because people kept setting me up."

"I dated a few guys at college. No one I really liked."

"Well, that's good. I was worried that you were going to tell me you were engaged."

Claudia smiled in spite of herself. "No, nothing ever went that far." Then she got angry. "Wait a minute! You mean that you allowed my father to convince you in one short conversation, that you should just drop me? I went off to college thinking you had suddenly stopped loving me! Or if my mother was right, that you were playing around behind my back the entire time, and that my wanting to go to college had given you the excuse you needed to stop seeing me and focus on someone else." She stabbed a piece of meat and stuck it in her mouth, and chewed furiously, glaring.

Jeff glared back. "Hey! I'm one of the victims here! How do you think it felt to be told that you're worthless and that to be chivalrous, you should just get out of the way so that the woman you love more than anything in the world can go find someone better!"

"You, a victim?" Claudia whispered angrily. But then her eyes filled with tears and she asked, "You loved me more than anything in the world?"

"Yes," Jeff admitted. "I really did." He laid his hand upon hers. "Claudia, I'd like to start over, without any help from your parents."

"I don't know if I can go back."

"No, of course, we can't. We've both changed a lot since then. But we can give ourselves another chance together." Jeff didn't like the pleading tone in his voice. But he had been thinking about this for too long not to just keep going.

"Do you think we can do it?"

"I want to try, Claudia." He gazed earnestly into her eyes. "I've missed you so much."

"I missed you too."

Jeff exhaled for the first time in what seemed like a long time. He smiled in relief.

"Can you eat yet? I really wanted you to like this place."

"I can try." Claudia shakily raised a bite of meat to her lips. She chewed for a while, then she put her fork down again. "Tell me how your family is."

Jeff tried valiantly to speak in a normal tone of voice while he related the latest news about his mother and father, and his younger brother. When he finished with his stories, he glanced at her full plate of food and suggested, "Maybe you can take that home in a doggie bag?"

"Yes, it will make a delicious lunch tomorrow, I'm sure."

Finished with his own meal, Jeff folded his napkin neatly and laid it down beside his dish. Several servers quickly descended on them to clear the table, and someone else offered them coffee and dessert.

Jeff hesitated before he said, "We brought my parents here for their twenty-fifth anniversary last summer."

"How nice!" She looked around appreciatively. "This place is very special to you, then."

"Yes, they really enjoyed it." Jeff dumped several packets of sugar into his coffee and stirred. Claudia, watching him, added some sugar to her own cup. "Tell me about your family too, Claudia. How is your sister, Zoë? I think I met her once, but didn't get to talk to her very much. And what about your brother? How is he doing now?"

"Benjamin? He's doing fine." She tasted the sweet coffee, and made a face. Jeff passed her the cream.

"Maybe you'll like it this way."

"Thanks." She sipped again, and nodded. "A little better."

"You're not really a coffee drinker, are you?"

"No, not really." She took another sip and then pushed it away, laughing a little bit. "I don't know why I ordered it."

Jeff leaned forward. "You don't have to drink coffee just because I like it. What would you rather have?" He waved for the waiter to return.

Claudia blushed. "Maybe some hot chocolate?"

That taken care of, Jeff returned to the conversation. "What's Benjamin like these days?"

"Well, you know, he's the smart one in the family. Actually, my parents have always said that he's a genius. He skipped a couple of grades early on. Later, they were always having to fight with the schools to challenge him more. Now he's in medical school, heading into his internship year. Don't get the wrong impression, though. He's not a snob."

"That's good. But did your parents really put it that way? That he's 'the smart one?'" Jeff was incredulous.

"Well, it was just obvious that he was," she squirmed uncomfortably. "I am relatively successful when I study very hard, but Benjamin was just gifted. I don't mind!"

"You've also been very successful, from what I've seen. Haven't you? Didn't you have mostly As all through your senior year in high school? And how did you do in college?"

"I had As there too. But I had to work really hard."

"I bet your brother works hard too, doesn't he?"

"Yes, he does. He studies all the time."

"I rest my case. You don't give yourself enough credit."

"You rest your case? You rest your case?" Claudia was suddenly livid. "Don't you ever argue with me like you're some hot shot lawyer who can't ever accept that I might have an intelligent thought in my own head! I get enough of that at home."

Jeff was taken aback. She had a point though. He had chosen his words poorly. "You're right. I should not have argued with you about your brother. I'm sorry. I won't ever do it again."

* * *

Claudia was shocked at herself. Here she was, finally with Jeff again after having missed him so desperately for so long. And now, she had screamed at him like a banshee. He would probably never call her again. Suddenly, tears were falling down her cheeks.

"I'm sorry," she blubbered. "I don't usually talk like this…" Then she noticed he was actually apologizing and handing her his handkerchief. She sniffed as she wiped her eyes.

"I'm really sorry. Don't be mad at me. I'll be nice."

Claudia couldn't help but laugh at Jeff's puppy eyes.

"I can't believe I blew up like that. I don't think you deserved that."

"Well, I was acting like a jerk. You're allowed to call me on it."

"I think I'm more angry at my parents. I should be screaming at them instead of you."

"I'd sure like to see that. You can practice on me if you want."

Jeff was such a dear. Claudia couldn't help but love him.

They watched as the waiter set a dish of crème brulée and a bowl of hazelnut gelato on the table. "Shall we share?"

Even though she had barely eaten any, the pork chop was sitting heavily on Claudia's stomach. She wasn't sure that she could enjoy anything after the roller coaster of emotions that she had just experienced. She gazed at her dessert brooding. *He said he loved me more than anything in the world.* Her eyes brimmed over with tears again, and she looked up at Jeff. *He deserves another chance.*

She took a taste of the gelato. *How luscious!* Claudia knew Jeff's eyes were on her as she swooned over the bit of Italian iced heaven, but it wasn't worth trying to be poised and in control. She finally came up for air. "You're not eating."

He smiled and obediently picked up his spoon. "I couldn't take my eyes off of you. Haven't you ever had ice cream before?" After one bite of his own creamy dessert, Claudia had a good laugh watching him race his way through it. Before he took the last bite, she whisked his plate away and replaced it with the last bite of gelato. They finished slowly, their eyes on each other now. All shyness was gone.

At the end of the evening, promptly at ten o'clock, since they decided there was no sense in perturbing Claudia's father more than necessary, Jeff pulled the car up in front of Claudia's house. They sat there in the dark, their hands entwined. Finally, Jeff pulled Claudia to him and gently kissed her on the lips. She closed her eyes and sighed. Though she sank into the kiss completely, it was over much too soon, and she was out of the car waving goodbye to Jeff, hoping that she would see him again as soon as possible.

She let herself in through the front door, trying hard to hold on to the feeling of Jeff's strong hands on her shoulders.

"Well, you took your time, I see," her father's voice came from the large leather armchair in the corner of the darkened living room.

"I'm sorry, Dad. I hoped this was early enough that I wouldn't disturb you when I came in."

"It's been a long hard day for me. I'm ready to turn in."

"I'm tired too. I think I'll go straight to bed."

Her father rose and turned off the lamp. He turned to Claudia, "Tony Emerson tells me that he offered you a position at the firm. You can drive in with me tomorrow to fill out the paperwork and get started."

"But I haven't decided whether to take the job yet. I have many other applications out there already. I want to see whether any of them are going to come through."

"Claudia, an offer in a prestigious firm like this one is not easy to come by and Mr. Emerson is doing our family a great favor by extending it. This is better than anything else you're likely to find. You should accept it."

Claudia felt helpless to contradict her father. Tears threatened to squeeze through her lids, so she turned to go up the stairs.

"I'll be ready to leave at eight a.m. sharp." He called up after her. "Don't be late."

CHAPTER 8

Early the next morning, Claudia stood at the front door of her home, dressed trimly in a gray suit, and carrying a small briefcase. "Bye Mom," she called toward the kitchen. No reply came, but her father was tapping insistently on the horn out in the driveway, so she hurried out the door.

The ride to the office was quiet. Her father didn't look at her when she climbed into the smoky gray Cadillac. While he drove, he concentrated on the road without speaking. Outside the window, people on the streets were arriving at work, greeting each other and laughing. Claudia sighed, wondering whether this was going to be a typical day from now on.

"I hope you remember that you're representing the family now. These people look up to me. I expect you to make me proud."

"I can handle myself."

"Be sure that you do."

Claudia looked at her hands in her lap and then looked up again. "I'm going to be getting my car from the mechanic at noon, Dad. You won't need to drive me home tonight." Taking a chance she said, "And I think I'd like to drive myself to work every day. I'll be more flexible if I have my own transportation."

Her father frowned at her. "Don't you think that's a bit wasteful?"

"It's not a long drive. Sometimes I have errands to run."

"Well, we'll see. We don't need to decide right away." He pulled the car into his VIP spot in the parking lot of an ornately decorated building. They walked into the building together. Her father greeted everyone he passed. Claudia smiled in her turn, shaking hands with the few that her father took the time to introduce to her.

"This is your stop. Just wait for Mary to call you in, and you can tell her who you are and that you are to start work today. I have an appointment to go to."

Claudia watched him disappear around the corner. She turned toward the door he had indicated, but before she had a chance to knock, it opened. A cheerful, pretty woman in her forties motioned for her to enter.

"Hello, I'm Mary Arnold, the office manager. You must be Claudia Gilmore." She shook Claudia's hand firmly and motioned to the chair beside the desk.

"Yes, I am. Mr. Emerson told me to come and talk to you about a job, though I'm not exactly sure what it would entail."

"Here, let's get through this paperwork. After that, I can walk you around and introduce you to everyone, and show you what you'll be doing."

Claudia wished she felt like she had a choice in the matter. But if everyone else here was this pleasant, she might not really mind working here. She smiled back at Mary Arnold, and pulled out her pen.

Half an hour later, the collection of forms was sorted and bound in a fresh new manila folder with her name on it, and the two of them set off to walk around the building.

"As you know, this is one of the busiest law offices in the region. We have five full partners…"

With half her mind on Mary's narrative and the other half on Jeff, Claudia allowed herself to be led down the hall to her new office. Through open doors along the way, she saw desks and serious-looking young people, dressed identically in trim black suits, carrying piles of books and papers. A constant din of voices blended with the buzz of the fluorescent lights and the hum of the air conditioners.

"This office handles all sorts of legal issues including…"

Claudia watched her steps on the carpeted hallway. She studied the legal assistants, her own age, who all seemed to know where they were going. Mary stopped to knock on an office door. When she heard the muffled "Come in" she opened the door and indicated the man seated at the desk inside.

"Claudia, this is Nathan Emerson, one of our young trial lawyers. Barbara Johnson is his assistant. You'll meet her later."

The young man who rose from the large leather chair behind the massive oak desk was strikingly handsome, with piercing black eyes and equally black hair, thick and wavy, but styled neatly into a cut that signaled power and confidence.

"I'm glad to meet you Claudia," Nathan said as he took her hand. He squeezed it and held it a bit too long, while he gazed deep into her eyes.

With her hand trapped like that, she felt an uncomfortable intimacy in his eye contact. She turned to look at Mary Arnold, and tried to go on talking as though her hand were not still in his grip. "So, will I be working here for Mr. Emerson, Mary?"

Before Mary could reply, Nathan spoke. "Are you my new secretary? Excellent! I have a large backlog of work that I've been asking for help with. If it works out, you can stay permanently."

Claudia finally got her hand back, and turned to see Mary backing down the hall again with an amused smile.

* * *

By the middle of the day, Claudia was beginning to understand her job. Her own office was much smaller and less majestic than Nathan's, but it was almost directly across the hall so that he could drop by and give her paperwork or instructions at any time. She had to answer the phone and transfer calls to the other offices. Typing would take up much of her day. Using the word processing software on her computer would not be difficult, nor would learning all the formats for each of the types of documents she'd be producing. There really wasn't anything challenging about this work, but it didn't have anything to do with anthropology. At least it was a steady job, and she'd be earning some money. Now that her car was coming out of the shop, her search for an apartment could take a higher priority.

She thought about her new boss. Nathan Emerson was certainly a good-looking man, with his broad shoulders and the piercing gaze that looked right through you. He was a proud man, she could tell, and ambitious.

While she was sitting there musing about Nathan, the door to his office opened abruptly and he walked out of the room and past her door, brushing past a dark-haired, middle-aged woman who was just walking in. She had a blocky figure and was dressed in a no-nonsense black business suit and a pale blue blouse. She headed straight for the large table in the corner and set a pile of books and papers on an open space. She looked around the room and finally grabbed a blank sheet of paper out of Claudia's printer and a pen from her desk and sat down to write a note.

Finished, she handed the pen to Claudia and said, "Thanks. I'm Barbara Johnson, by the way."

"I'm glad to meet you. I'm Claudia. I just started today."

"Yes, I knew Nathan was asking for a new secretary. The last one left rather abruptly." Barbara peered into Claudia's eyes. "How have things been so far?"

"Very nice," Claudia stammered slightly. "I think I'll have no problem handling the work. Or at least, it doesn't seem very complicated yet."

"And…how are things with Nathan? How is he treating you?"

"I have nothing to complain about." Claudia replied. "Really, things are fine."

"That's good," Barbara looked toward the door and then leaned in to talk more softly. "Claudia, did you know that Nathan is Anthony Emerson's son?"

Claudia started, then flushed. "I suspected it, Barbara. Oh dear. Um. What does that mean?"

"Oh nothing. It's just something to keep in mind." They both heard the steps nearing the door. Barbara got up abruptly. "Don't hesitate to talk to me if anything bothers you at all." Then she was gone.

Claudia turned back to her work as Nathan came back in and sat down at his desk. So, Nathan was the son of one of the most senior partners at the firm. She thought about the times she had spoken with the older Emerson. The father's kind and gentle demeanor had apparently escaped the son. Instead, Nathan seemed hard, ambitious. Rather like her own father. And, if Barbara's intimations were correct, he could be someone to be wary of. It was interesting that she had landed in this job of all possible jobs at the firm, or in town for that matter. She wondered if her father had anything to do with that.

The day went by quickly. She picked up her car during the lunch hour and then sat outside in the courtyard eating her leftover lunch from last night's dinner. She had expected to be bored and watching the clock for the rest of the afternoon. But instead, the steady stream of small tasks that she was given easily filled up her time. She was surprised when the end of the workday arrived.

Later, walking through the lobby, Claudia saw Nathan and her father talking together. She tried to sneak out quietly, since they looked like they were deep in a serious conversation, but before she got to the door, she heard her father's voice calling her, "Claudia, come tell me how your first day went."

She turned and smiled brightly. "Hello! I think everything is going very smoothly."

"You know my new secretary, Mr. Gilmore?"

Claudia's father widened his eyes in pleasant surprise. "Why, I didn't know my daughter had been assigned to you. Claudia, you will find working for Mr. Emerson to be a very enriching experience."

"Yes, I can already tell that it's going to be interesting work." Claudia noticed with dismay how easily she played the role of the enthusiastic young new-hire that she knew her father expected. *Such pretention.*

She saw Nathan watching her with narrowed eyes. *I hope he can't read minds.* She looked back with the most convincing air of innocence that she could strike. Nathan put his arm around Claudia's shoulder. "I'm sure you'll be a great member of our team."

Claudia murmured her thanks and slipped away.

Walking to her car, she pulled out her cell phone to check for messages, and she noticed there was one text and a voicemail message. The text was from Andi, and the voicemail, from a number she did not recognize. She sat in her car and listened to the message.

"Hello Claudia, I hope this reaches you. This is Donna Spencer at the university in the anthropology department. Please give me a call. I'd like to talk to you about your senior paper and about your future."

Claudia hesitated then hit Save. Even though her job was going well enough, she didn't want to talk to her former mentor and instructor about how all her education was going out the window and how she was now a secretary typing up other people's papers, none of which had anything to do with what she had been doing in Dr. Spencer's lab.

She read Andi's text, "party my apt sat night. lots of friends: Naomi, Jeff…call me." Claudia smiled, and wrote it in her date book. She looked at her phone considering whether to return the other call. She sighed then dropped the phone back in her purse, started the car and drove away.

CHAPTER 9

The air was heavy with humidity as Claudia parked the car and walked into the house.

"Hi, Mom."

"Hello." Her mother paused from assembling her lasagna just long enough to brush the hair from her eyes. "I could use some help here. Would you start the salad while I finish this?"

"Wow, Mom, lasagna!" Claudia exclaimed. "Is it a special occasion?"

"Not really, Claudia. Your father likes to have a nice meal at dinnertime. I like to give him a reason to come home." Her mother looked up, eyes wide, then gave an unconvincing little laugh. She went back to concentrating on her work layering hot slippery noodles with the cheese mixture and the spicy red sauce together in the pan. Claudia opened the oven door while her mother slid the heavy pan in and then set the timer.

Claudia thought her mother looked tired and preoccupied.

"It smells delicious, Mom." Claudia smiled encouragingly.

"Well, thank you dear." Under her breath she said, "I hope he thinks so." She wiped her hands on her apron. Then, as though waking up, she said, "Why don't you finish that salad, Claudia?" As she turned to leave the room, she said over her shoulder, "When you're done, could you wipe up the kitchen a bit? I need to go make a phone call and straighten myself up. You will be here for dinner, won't you?" And she was gone.

With a sigh, Claudia turned to her salad making. Her mother seemed troubled. This side of her mother was unfamiliar to Claudia. Maybe she had finally grown up enough that she could see things she had never seen before. Or maybe this was something new. Could it be that her mother was just as uncertain of her father's love and approval as Claudia was herself? For the first time in her life, Claudia felt sympathy for her hard-working mother.

She finished chopping the vegetables for the meal's salad and then dampened a towel to lay over the greens so that they would not wilt before it was time to eat. Then, she put extra energy into wiping the counters clean and washing up the bowls and pans that were sitting in the sink awaiting cleanup. Finally the kitchen was sparkling, and she could see that there was another twenty minutes left on the timer. Claudia ran up the stairs to change for dinner.

When she heard the timer go off, she came back down to find her mother pulling the lasagna—its cheese nicely browned—out of the oven and onto a rack to cool. While the rest of the family was washing their hands and sitting down at the table, Claudia dressed the salad and gave it a good toss before handing it to her father.

"Would you like a glass of wine, Roger?"

"Of course, Annette. Is there a Chianti open yet?"

"Yes, I opened the 2006 bottle about an hour ago. It should taste good by now, don't you think?" Claudia's mother smiled into her husband's eyes. There was no more hint of the fatigue or resignation that Claudia thought she saw earlier.

As the wine was being served around the table, Zoë skittered around the corner of the hallway and threw herself into her seat, joining the rest of the family.

"Can I have some too?" Zoë started to rise, heading for the china cabinet where the glassware was stored.

Her mother picked up an extra glass she had at her side. "Yes, don't get up, Zoë. I've got a glass for you here." She poured Zoë a small amount and then took a sip from her own.

Zoë rolled her eyes and gulped the wine down like it was fruit juice. It was gone in just a few swallows, and Zoë immediately held her glass out for more.

"Wait a while, Zoë! I'll give you more when the rest of the family is ready for a second glass."

"But Mom, you didn't give me enough!"

"Honey, you drink too quickly. You should savor it."

This produced another roll of the eyes from Zoë, which got a glare from her father. Claudia cringed, but miraculously, neither of them pushed the issue. Everyone was quiet for a while, working on their lasagna. The sound of forks scraped on the plates, everyone was chewing and swallowing, and the melted cheese concoction slowly disappeared from the pan. The gooey cheese, the thick layer of beef and sausage, and the béchamel sauce between the layers of noodles and ricotta could not help but take everyone's attention for at least a while. The salad made its rounds too, which provided a fresh and crunchy alternative to the hot main dish. The wine was poured two more times before the bottle was empty, and even Zoë finally got her glass filled completely at the end, when her mother was draining the bottle's last drop.

"Wow, Mom," Benjamin said as he leaned back finally. "That was magnificent."

"Thank you, Benjamin."

"Yes, delicious," "Really good, Mom," "Thanks, Mom," came a chorus of comments from the rest of the family.

"Now, who wants ice cream?"

Claudia jumped up to help her mother clear the lasagna away and bring in the dessert. While they busied themselves in the kitchen, Claudia's father decided to direct the dinner conversation. "Zoë, tell me how your classes are coming along."

"Just like always, Dad." Zoë frowned. "Boring as usual."

Claudia, dishing up ice cream in the kitchen, held her breath for the explosion.

"You need a better attitude than that, Zoë!" Her father's fingers tapped on the table.

"Dad, can't you stay off my case for just one day?" Zoë slammed down her napkin and got up from the table just as Claudia and her mother came in with the ice cream.

"Zoë, don't you want some dessert?"

"No, Mom, maybe later." Zoë left the room.

Claudia and Benjamin looked at each other silently. Their mother sighed.

Without a target for his frustration, their father looked around the table angrily. His eyes lit upon Claudia. "You could help a little more around here too, Claudia."

"What else should I be doing?"

"Didn't your mother ask you to step in with your sister? You did nothing while she talked back to me."

"Dad, I wouldn't feel comfortable joining in with your conversation."

"Well, we need to show a united front with her. She's completely out of control, and if she thinks you are on her side, she'll never listen to reason."

"Dad, I don't know what it is you want me to help you talk her into."

Her mother broke in, saying brightly, "Here Roger, I have your favorite flavor of ice cream." She handed him his bowl and then passed some to the others. The four of them began eating, and the conversation became more polite, but also more distant.

"So Claudia, tell us about your day."

"It was nice, Mom. I'm going to be working for one of the trial lawyers in the firm. I think it will be interesting."

"That's nice, dear. And Benjamin?"

Grateful not to have the attention on her, Claudia listened to Benjamin recite his actions of the day: what he studied, where he went for lunch, and what his professors said to him.

Finally, her father folded his napkin and placed it on the table, got up and left the room. Benjamin murmured something about going to the library and left. Before Claudia knew it, she was back in the kitchen cleaning, and her mother had disappeared too. This new routine was already getting old.

Heading up to her room later, she contemplated grabbing her keys and going out for a drive, but then she saw Zoë peek out from around her bedroom door. "Claudia, do you want to come in and sit awhile?"

"Sure," she slipped inside. She settled herself on the foot of the bed while Zoë leaned back on her pillows. "Why are we sneaking around?"

"Because Mom and Dad want you to come and *talk* to me, and I don't want them to think they're winning."

Claudia smiled broadly. "Maybe we could pretend to have a fight. That would show them, wouldn't it?"

Zoë laughed, her face opening up. "It sure would. We can reserve that for later, when you go back to your room. In the meantime, I want to know more about your first day at work. Was it very horrible working with Dad?"

"There were definitely some weird moments, like driving in together. But mostly I never saw him. He was off doing whatever he was doing, and I was in a totally different part of the building. Everybody was nice, and the work isn't hard. I think I will be able to do just fine." Her face clouded. "I just don't know that I want to do this job for the rest of my life. I really did think that I was going to college for a reason."

"Well, I know that Dad was really mad when you told him you were going to graduate school. He railed around the house for days —yelling about spending all that money on you, and how you hadn't even chosen anything worthwhile to study. I had to just avoid them both during that time."

"Wow. I'm so sorry! I really thought that it was my decision to make and that it wouldn't matter that much to them. It's my life, isn't it?"

"Of course, *I* think that! But Dad doesn't. Haven't you noticed yet that Dad thinks he owns us and that our job is just to do and be whatever he tells us to?"

"But, I thought I *was* doing what he wanted me to do: I studied hard, I got good grades, I impressed my professors, I was accepted into graduate school. And he's still not proud of me."

Claudia reclined on the bed and supported her head on her hand. The pleasant mood was gone. "I just can't seem to please him."

"Welcome to my world, Claudia," Zoë said bitterly. "He never looks at me without thinking of something negative to say."

Claudia met Zoë's eyes and held her gaze without speaking. Zoë broke the silence first. "I know. I'm not trying very hard, am I? But look at you! You try all the time, and he still doesn't like you much. So, heck with it. That's what I say."

"Well, a little effort might at least get Mom and Dad off your case. And sometimes I think you work so hard to push their buttons that you hurt yourself more than you hurt them."

"What do you mean by that?" Zoë picked angrily at a thread on her comforter.

Claudia thought a moment and then decided to just dive in. "One of my friends told me that she saw you with some guys who might be pushing drugs. It makes me worry too."

Zoë sighed heavily. "You just don't know what it's like for me. I'm not popular like you were in high school. The 'good' kids don't give me the time of day. The kids I hang around with really aren't so bad. They understand me and a lot of the stuff I put up with here at home."

"I just don't want you hurting yourself," Claudia said, finally letting her concern show. "And I'd really like to see you on better terms with Mom and Dad."

"I don't see any hope for that."

"It does seem impossible sometimes. Maybe I can help you think of some strategies you could put to use."

"Claudia, this whole family is all about strategies. Don't you ever get tired of that?"

"I...I don't really think of it like that. I just want peace."

"But when you work so hard for peace, don't you think you lose yourself? I think I'd have to be someone totally different from who I am for them to ever be satisfied with me."

Her sister's bluntness made her think. Here she had been admiring her friend Andi for being herself no matter who she was with, when she herself worked so hard to be someone different just to get along.

"You're a pure flame," she whispered.

"What? What's that?"

"You can be yourself, even with all sorts of different people. That takes a special kind of person, Zoë."

"Well thanks. I think. Though I'm not sure that's a good thing. It would be nice if I could stop irritating Mom and Dad at least."

"Well, I seem to be able to do that to some extent. Maybe if you teach me how to be myself, I can teach you how to get along."

"Can you get the folks to quit nagging me about every little thing?"

"It might take some work, but it should be possible. Of course, I'm not always very good at it either."

Zoë sighed. "No guarantees, huh?"

"No. But imagine, if you suddenly became the model child, it might put them off balance and maybe they'd be so dazed, they'd forget to criticize."

"Me? The model child? Ha! That'd be the day."

"Like I said, it's just one strategy among many. It can't hurt, can it?"

Zoë sat and thought for a while, then laughed. "Maybe it's worth a try, eh? What should I do?"

They talked a while longer, Claudia handing down all the ideas she'd ever had in her own effort to gain their parents' favor. Later, Claudia wondered how long Zoë could keep up the motivation to work on being someone their parents could approve of. She knew from her own experience the difficulty of pleasing their mother and father, but they were the only parents they had, and they couldn't go on with the way things were now. Tomorrow would be an interesting day.

Chapter 10

The rest of the week Claudia felt as if she was running the gauntlet. Every time she turned around, it seemed, there was a new challenge to face or another person on the verge of panic asking her to somehow calm the world down and get everybody's lives back in balance. She found herself thinking in terms of myths and fairy tales—that it was she who had her finger in the dike, holding back the flood waters from the northern ocean, or that she had the weight of the entire globe resting on her shoulders.

She hadn't yet had the nerve to return her teacher's phone call. She would love to talk with Dr. Spencer again, but she felt trapped by events here at home and was ashamed of that feeling. She didn't see how she could admit to her professor that she wasn't returning to go to graduate school because her father wouldn't let her. Even if she were to somehow defy her father, she worried about both her sister and her mother. Perhaps if she stayed, she could help them in some way.

She knew something was up with her mother, but she never got another glimpse into whatever it was she almost saw the other day. She found herself watching her father at work. He never allowed any concerns to show on his face. Since they were driving separately now, she saw him in the morning as they left, and then again at dinner time. He treated her coldly, almost as a punishment for her not wanting to ride in with him. She tried not to let it bother her. She was smothered already. By the time she got home from work, she had just enough time to help with dinner and then clean up afterward, talk to Zoë, and then get to bed early so she could be well rested the next day.

She had to hand it to Zoë. Zoë was putting in a lot more effort on the home front. Her alarm was waking her up good and early, and she was getting clean and dressed and down for breakfast in time to sit with the entire family. At first, their parents would glare at Zoë when she walked into the room, as though they were certain she had just done something terribly wrong. But, Claudia's hand on Zoë's arm seemed to help her stay calm through this transition period, and now the scowls were diminishing. Instead, Zoë was being ignored as much as Claudia usually was, which Claudia preferred to think was an improvement, though she thought a little positive attention would have been welcome. Zoë was becoming less likely to roll her eyes at everything their parents said, unless it was truly irresistible, and then she would hide her face behind her hand and make her faces for Claudia alone. Claudia thought of that as an improvement too, and she rewarded Zoë by laughing about it with her late in the evening during their sisterly chats.

She knew that though Zoë was dressed demurely at the breakfast table and left the house with a clean, fresh-scrubbed face, she was carrying her freakier accessories and makeup in her backpack so she could don her cynical persona as soon as she was outside of her parents' view. Claudia didn't fight it. Change is hard. Her best bet was probably to convince Zoë to look forward to college as a good place to rework her image.

Work was going smoothly, though Claudia suspected that she would never be very enthusiastic about typing and filing. She found that the location of her desk meant that she was isolated from all the other office workers at her level in the organization, so she was not getting to know anybody else. The legal assistant who worked for Nathan was friendly, and Claudia appreciated their brief conversations. Nathan himself was usually in a hurry, on his way to meetings or to court or in his office with the door closed, so there was no talking with him about anything not having to do with work. Not that she had any reason to expect anything more, nor did she even want it. But she contrasted it with life in Dr. Spencer's lab where she was always in the middle of stimulating conversations and felt appreciated for her contributions.

She sometimes felt Nathan's gaze on her. When she looked up from her desk, he'd be standing in the doorway, and their eyes would lock together. But then he would swirl around on his heel and be gone. It was strange, but she felt a tingle when it happened. Though he didn't make any explicit moves in her direction, she had the distinct impression that he was flirting with her. One step here, one step there, almost like a silent dance, underlying everything else that was happening in their days.

She wasn't sure how she felt about Nathan. He was a handsome man, one who would someday be a powerful partner in the same law firm as her father. In fact, he was similar to her father in many ways, which was enough to make her wary of his motives for the attention he paid to her. Her father never seemed to do anything unless it was going to help him get ahead or benefit in some way.

One day, Claudia was sitting at the corner deli eating her lunch when she felt her cell phone vibrate. Pulling it out, she found another message from Dr. Spencer. She must have missed the call when it came.

"I'd like to talk to you about some ideas I have about your future. Please call me at…" Claudia quickly copied the number in her date book and then listened to the message again. Her heart was pounding with nervousness. She knew it was time to return Dr. Spencer's call. She shouldn't have left it so long. Besides, maybe she had some good news. She hated to get her hopes up, but this might just be exactly what she had been wishing for.

She dialed the number.

"Claudia. Thank you so much for calling back. I have a proposal for you. I don't know how settled you are back at home already, or what you're doing, but…"

"Well, I did just start a new job, but I would still like to hear what you have to say. I had a hard time finding anything in my field."

"Forgive me if I am wrong, but I was wondering if you were concerned about the cost of graduate school. I wish you had brought it up with me earlier in the year, but I don't think it is too late, even now. I have a five-year grant that covers the funding for several of my assistants in the lab. You remember that Yoon Ji finished in the spring?"

Claudia caught her breath. "Yes, I remember."

"I've worked out the numbers and I believe you would be pleased to know that I can offer you a stipend that should cover your living expenses, and enough to travel home a few times a year. I would also arrange to have your tuition waived, so you would be a full-time student."

"Oh my goodness, what a generous offer! It seems too good to be true!"

"In fact, I've already spoken with the graduate admissions department, and they are saving you a spot."

"Wow. I would love to come work with you. This is just the kind of opportunity I was wishing for. I just have to figure out how to go about extracting myself from my current situation…"

"Please do whatever you need to do, but don't take too long. I can send you the forms now, in fact, if you want to get started on the paperwork."

"Thank you, please do. I will get back to you as soon as I can."

Claudia closed her cell phone and sat quietly humming with excitement. She felt like dancing. This was exactly what she was wishing for. Dr. Spencer's classes had been fascinating, and the experience she'd had working in the lab had been exhilarating. She loved the idea of doing it for money and for credit.

She looked up at the building where she and her father spent so many hours every day. She knew she didn't belong in that job. Why did her father care so much if she worked there? Sure, it was a steady paycheck, but it wasn't ever going to bring fulfillment.

Her father didn't seem terribly concerned about her fulfillment. Not even Benjamin felt free to aim that high. Prestige, that's what he was supposed to earn. And for some reason her father thought it was worth supporting Benjamin through medical school, but not Claudia through graduate school. Well, now he wouldn't have to pay for it, so he had no right to complain.

***

Claudia had to wait until dinnertime to make her announcement to her family. She mulled over how to approach the subject. She was still hurt by the "unskilled labor" comment that her father made the first day she was home. He just didn't understand anthropology. This offer should prove to him that she did have some skills that were valuable to someone. She hoped that he would be proud to hear how much her professor thought of her. She was rather proud herself.

She was nervous getting ready for dinner that night. She waited until everybody seemed to be in a good mood and then she began.

"Speaking of school, I have an announcement to make."

All eyes turned toward her. "I got a phone call the other day from a former professor of mine. We had a nice talk this afternoon."

Her mother smiled politely and said, "That's nice dear. Benjamin would you please pour me some water." Benjamin hurried to oblige, and her father and Zoë went back to poking at their plates.

"She offered me a job in her lab, and a scholarship to go to graduate school."

That got their attention.

Zoë, with a horrified expression, exclaimed, "But Claudia, you can't go away now. You only just got back!"

Her mother, glancing nervously at her husband, sat silently twisting her napkin in her hands.

Her father's smile disappeared. He slowly reached for the bowl of green beans and spooned some onto his plate. Then he took a bite, while the others waited for him to speak. He dabbed the corners of his mouth with his napkin and then placed it carefully back in his lap. Finally, he looked up and said with a hard look in his eyes, "Of course, you said no."

Claudia's voice shook, but she tried to stand her ground. "Why would I do that?" She hated the whine she heard in her own voice.

"Claudia," he spoke slowly and deliberately, as though to a small child. "We paid for you to go to that glorified finishing school, so you could play at being an intellectual for four years. We made space for you to move back in with us because you still didn't have any real skills, even though it's been a great imposition on us. I went out on a limb to get you a job in my own office, even though you showed no enthusiasm for the position. And now, even though there was no reason to think it would work out, I am told that you are slowly but surely becoming somewhat useful. What's more, the senior partner's son seems to like having you there. If you leave and go to graduate school, you'll just be back in four more years in the same situation you were in this summer, needing a job, and having no marketable skills. No. You do not have the option of quitting this job. You will stay, and continue to work hard, and if we're lucky, you will finally attract some young man who will marry you and get you out of this house once and for all."

Her father went back to stabbing dinner with his fork.

Her eyes growing wider and wider throughout this tirade, Claudia was ashamed to feel tears forming and trailing down her cheeks. Zoë gaped wordlessly, and Benjamin sat staring at his food. Claudia couldn't eat any longer. She finally stood up and walked out of the room.

She hated her tears. Why did she put up with such abuse? She had been a perfectly capable adult person but was now reduced to a sniveling child. Well, no more! She was going to get out of here, one way or the other.

CHAPTER 11

The end of the week finally arrived. Ever since the call from Dr. Spencer, Claudia had had a hard time concentrating on her work. She couldn't help but think of this job as a temporary placement even though her father had ordered her to refuse her teacher's offer. She hadn't called Dr. Spencer back, since she couldn't bear the thought of refusing the job of her dreams. Yet, she didn't see any hope for changing her father's mind either, and hadn't the nerve to openly disobey him.

Claudia felt like she desperately needed a break from the daily routine at the law office, and the time to see her friends again. Jeff had asked her to spend most of Saturday with him, and though she did not know what they were going to be doing, she was determined to enjoy herself. She woke up early, more from habit than because she had to, since Jeff wouldn't be picking her up until ten. She dressed quickly but carefully. Even though they had only just renewed their relationship, she wanted to look nice for him today.

She ate some breakfast, cleaned up, and was ready and waiting much too early, so she sat in the living room with the same novel she had been trying to read for several weeks now. As before, the minute she sat down to read, she was interrupted, this time by her father who had also gotten up early in the morning, and was now doing paperwork, probably for a case he was working on. They hadn't spoken more than two words to each other since he had put her so thoroughly in her place, but she was not willing to let him think she was going to just give in on everything.

Now, she looked up from her book and found him standing in the doorway looking at her. "Yes? Is there something you want?" She replaced the bookmark again and stared steadily at her father.

"I hope you have dropped the idea of going back to college, Claudia. You do understand that it isn't the right thing for you."

"No, Dad, I do not. I think that I'm the one who should make the decisions about what is best for me."

"You're still very young. You don't know what's best for you."

"I disagree. And I doubt whether working as a secretary in your law office for the rest of my life is what's best for me."

"I don't expect this to be for the rest of your life. Your mother isn't still a secretary is she?"

"No, she married you and quit her job. Are you expecting me to do the same? I'm not sure I should be expected to follow in her footsteps. I have my own interests and my own goals."

Claudia was surprised at herself. She had never spoken that way to her father before. She checked her watch. "I liked the work I was doing at the university. And I was good at it. I wasn't just 'unskilled labor.'"

Jeff's car pulled up in front of the house. Before her father could respond, she grabbed her purse and headed for the front door. "Good bye, Dad. I'm going out with Jeff today." She flew through the door and slammed it shut.

* * *

Jeff watched Claudia run down the sidewalk, her curls bouncing, and her strained expression becoming a smile as she approached the car. She moved well, with an easy rhythm about her. During high school she had spent her summers at the swimming quarry. He often watched her doing laps, completely comfortable in the water, floating, doing porpoise dives, or just playing. When she was on his motorcycle with him, her body almost became an extension of his own. She leaned with him on the turns, and lowered her head into the wind when he went fast down the country roads. Riding full throttle was exhilarating for him, and she seemed to love it just as much.

Jeff jumped out of the car just in time to open her door for her. Back in the driver's seat, he glanced up at the house before he drove away. Seeing Mr. Gilmore at the window looking out at him, he leaned across Claudia and waved toward the window.

"Next time you should pick me up on the motorcycle." Claudia grumbled as she glared back toward the house.

"You're feeling rather contrary today." Jeff grinned.

Claudia laughed. "So are you, I see! He probably didn't think you'd notice he was there." She sighed and said, "Let's not think about my parents. They are such a puzzle." Her smile transformed her face.

Jeff reached for her hand. Her hand felt so soft and delicate in his. He stole a glance at her while he drove. She looked troubled.

"What is it?"

She opened her mouth as though to say something. Then she looked out the window.

"It's nothing. Let's just enjoy the day."

They sat there in silence while he drove.

"Where are we going Jeff?" Claudia finally said as they reached the edge of town and kept going.

"It's a surprise. I'm going to show you who I am these days. And we'll see how much you like it. And that's all I'm going to say." He pressed his lips together to prove it.

"All right, we'll just see. I hope it's not too weird." She grimaced at him, but there was a twinkle in her eyes too. Finally they pulled up to a huge bunker-like building made of cement block, in what seemed like the middle of nowhere. They got out of the car, and Claudia stretched to get the kinks out of her back. Jeff caught his breath at the sight of her sweater clinging to the curve of her breasts. It was all he could do to resist grabbing her right there in the parking lot. He knew that it was an unconscious gesture, but didn't she know she was driving him crazy?

"We go in this way," Jeff said, leading the way to a heavy metal door around the side of the building. "Wait. You're going to need one of these." He dug into the bag he was carrying and pulled out two sets of large plastic and foam ear muffs. He put one pair on his own head. Then he handed her the other, showing her how to adjust them. Thus outfitted, they walked through the door.

* * *

Claudia looked around. The long empty cement space looked like an unfinished basement. Ahead of her, she caught a glimpse of numerous figures dressed in camouflage, some kneeling, some standing at tables in a row leading away from the door. Suddenly a cacophony of sound came from inside the building, and she clapped her hands over her ears, which she remembered were covered by the ear muffs that Jeff had given her to put on. She had unconsciously backed up toward the door when the noise began, but then she looked up and noticed Jeff calmly moving toward a desk in the corner by the door. Quickly she lowered her hands, gripped her purse by her side, and followed him, trying to look like she knew what she was doing.

Jeff helped her fill out some registration forms and then led Claudia to a table at one end of the room. She watched in amazement as he placed his pack on the table, and began pulling several handguns and boxes of ammunition out of it. He laid them carefully on the table, motioning to her to watch what he was doing.

Claudia had never been this close to a firearm. It was fascinating to see Jeff take each one, load it full of bullets, and then set them down again on the table. By the time he was done setting everything up, the noise had subsided. She saw that many of the targets were now sliding on runners toward the front of the room, and the shooters were replacing them with new ones. Taking advantage of the relative silence, Jeff pushed his ear muffs down on his neck and motioned for Claudia to do the same.

"I'm going to do one round of shooting and you can watch. I'd like you to try it yourself, but not until I have explained all the safety rules to you. When you're ready, I can give you this nice light handgun that I think you'll be able to fire without too much kickback. Once you learn how to squeeze and shoot, nice and steady, I think you'll be able to shoot any of these guns here."

Claudia couldn't understand how Jeff could speak in such a matter-of-fact way. Just watching him, so comfortable in this environment, gave her a shiver of fear. But she was thrilled at the idea that she would have a gun in her hand soon. He just had time to point out some basics, and then there was some signal that Claudia didn't notice, and all the noise started up again. She popped her ear muffs back on as fast as she could, and clasped her hands in excitement as Jeff picked up the largest of the handguns and started shooting.

She lost count of how many times Jeff fired the pistol, but when the one he was holding was empty, he picked up the next one and started shooting. He stopped before the rest of the room quieted down, and began reloading, taking his time, waiting for the period of silence so he could go on with his tutorial. In this next lesson, Claudia learned the parts of the semi-automatic handgun: the cylinder, the safety, the magazine, the cartridges, and how they all worked. Before long, the invisible signal went off and everybody was at it again.

While Jeff was doing his target practice this time, Claudia studied the other shooters. Most of them were men, but there were some women among them, serious women, dressed in jeans and t-shirts, or camouflage, like some of the men. They seemed so strong and sure of themselves. They made an interesting group of people. She couldn't imagine meeting any of them at the law office where she now spent the bulk of her time. But then, she didn't feel like she belonged there either, so it didn't really bother her. Some of the others were in groups, or in pairs, with one person shooting and the other loading the guns. As she was staring at each one in turn, she was suddenly surprised to find an amused pair of eyes staring back. She flushed, but then the face around those eyes wrinkled into a grin and the man winked at her. His companion put his gun down and Claudia's new friend turned his back to her again.

She went back to watching Jeff reload his guns. Seeing her attention on him, he took her trembling hand and showed her how to push the cartridges down into the magazine until it couldn't hold any more. Then he demonstrated the position of his hands, with one on the grip of the pistol, and the other around it for support and stability. When it was quiet enough to hear again, he showed her how to lay her trigger finger up alongside the barrel when not actually shooting to avoid accidentally putting a bullet in her foot. After replacing the target, which had become so full of holes it was almost in tatters, Jeff asked Claudia if she was ready to try it herself.

This time, Claudia noticed the light at the end of the row turned from red to green, and then everybody picked up their guns to start shooting. Jeff showed her where to place her feet, and then he selected the smallest and the lightest of the pistols for her. She placed her hands exactly as he had shown her, while he watched closely to make sure that her finger was in place on the side of the gun. Then he helped her stretch her elbows almost straight so that the gun was far from her face. She looked past the sights on the barrel of the gun and saw the target beyond them. She looked to Jeff for confirmation. He nodded. She moved her finger to the trigger and squeezed.

The gun recoiled upward in response to the explosion. It was surprising but not painful, thank goodness, so she looked at Jeff for her next cue. He nodded. She laughed with happiness and then suppressed her emotions and addressed the target once again. Taking careful aim, and knowing now what was going to happen, she pulled the trigger again and again. The target was far enough away that she wasn't certain how she was doing, but she felt that she was getting the hang of the physical act of standing in position and firing. In fact, she found herself concentrating so hard that she didn't notice the light turning red again. Jeff touched her arm and she stopped.

Claudia was exhilarated. "I love this! Let's see how I did!"

Jeff showed her how to push the button to bring the target up for their inspection. She was gratified to see that there were actually a few holes in it, though they were nowhere near the center, and she knew that she had shot many more times than the number of holes she counted.

"Hey, look at that! I hit it."

"You did great! Not very many people can hit the target on their first day shooting."

"Can I shoot some more?" she pleaded. "I think I can do better now."

"You're not tired yet?"

"No. I can go again, I'm sure. Help me load, okay?"

"No, you do it yourself now."

With Jeff watching closely, Claudia removed the magazine, and with the box of cartridges he handed her, she filled it up, and then, keeping the gun carefully pointing in the right direction, popped the magazine back into the gun like a pro. There was a hum of anticipation in her body, as she turned her head to see the others reloading and putting their targets back in place.

"Jeff, the target!"

"Don't worry." Jeff quickly switched it out and pushed the button to swing it away again.

The light turned green and Claudia took a deep breath, lifted her arms and again began firing. The rest of the morning, she repeated these actions over and over. She never lost that wonderful feeling of strength and excitement that holding and firing the handgun gave her. But her arms finally began to tire, so she sat to the side while Jeff wrapped up their session by doing a few more rounds himself.

As they were packing up to go, the gray-haired man who had winked at her stopped on his own way out to pat her on the shoulder. "You did some good shootin', little girl," he said with a friendly smile. "We'd better reserve a table for you from now on, hmm?"

Claudia shone with happiness. "I hope so. That was wonderful fun."

CHAPTER 12

All through the afternoon, Claudia held on to that wonderful powerful feeling that she had had while at the shooting range with Jeff. It was quiet at home, but she kept herself busy, straightening up her room and laundering her work clothes. She grabbed the newspaper to browse for apartments, but her heart wasn't in it and she found herself staring at the wallpaper but seeing nothing.

It bothered her that she hadn't yet told Jeff about her going back to grad school. She knew he would support her. He was so sweet that way. But somehow she also wanted to see where their relationship could go without anything distracting. The thought of her leaving could very well interfere with that.

"Hey Claudia." Zoë entered the dining room where Claudia had her newspapers spread on the table.

"Hey! What are you up to?"

"Just hanging out." Zoë read over Claudia's shoulder. "Two-bedroom apartment in the center of town. Hmmm, looks good. I can come spend the night now and then. Even better, I can move in with you and cook your meals."

Claudia laughed. "I could actually see you doing that." She turned to the apartment ads for the first time. "I think you need to finish high school before you move into an apartment."

"Why?" Zoë insisted. "I have some savings. I could afford at least a few months. I could get a job on the weekends."

Claudia looked at Zoë thoughtfully. "That's not actually an unthinkable idea. But I may not be here."

"You're really leaving then?"

"Yes. You know it's the right thing to do, even though Dad disapproves."

Zoë humphed. "He disapproves of everything."

"But Zoë, don't you think things are getting better? I haven't heard a real altercation between you in several days now."

Zoë looked at her under lowered eyebrows. "Is that really how you judge whether things are good or not?"

"No, not really. But it is a sign of improvement, and I'm not willing to write it off as hopeless."

"Claudia, things are only improving in your eyes because I've stopped showing any personality at all in this house. The only way to get him to stop yelling is to be completely silent and invisible. I watched you do it for years, and now you're trying to make me do it. I'm only doing it for you, you know, and also because I sort of wondered if it was possible. But it's not going to last forever."

Claudia looked at Zoë in shock. She was sometimes amazed at the perceptiveness of this younger sister of hers. She felt tears form.

Zoë grinned and gave Claudia a playful punch on the arm, "Hey listen. I'm going to save my money for when you let me move in with you wherever you are. I think I'll look for a job too. Do you have the 'help wanted' section?"

Claudia handed it over and watched Zoë while she looked over the ads.

"Do you really have time to work a job and study for your classes? That's not just something that Mom and Dad care about, you know. It really is important."

"I am studying. But sometimes my classes are just too hard, and I don't know what those crazy teachers even want."

"I could look over your work with you and help you figure out how to study," Claudia offered, then with a twinkle, "unless you're afraid that it's contrary to your real nature."

Zoë looked up from her newspaper and glared. "I would actually love to be better at that. Would you really help me? You're not too busy going out with your friends or getting ready to leave again?"

Claudia realized suddenly how alone Zoë must have felt during these last four years. Claudia and Benjamin had both been gone at school studying. And during all that time Zoë had been the child under the microscope. The pressure must have been unbearable. Not only had Zoë been an only child for the last four years, but she was just not naturally as good a student as either of her older siblings, so she would incur more of their parents' disapproval than they had. No wonder she was doing so poorly, at school and at home.

"Of course I'll help you, at least, as long as I'm home. I'm sorry I haven't been around for you."

"Really?" Zoë's face beamed. "Can I go get my books now?"

Claudia looked at her watch. "Sure, I have about an hour before I go to Andi's place for her party. Let's spend that hour on your studies, and then tomorrow, I'll give you all afternoon."

Zoë turned her face away, but Claudia could see her disappointment. "I promise. I will save the entire afternoon for you. Go get your books, and we'll make a plan."

Zoë gave a big sigh, and left the room. Soon she was back with a huge stack of textbooks. "I brought them all home, but I just don't know where to start."

For the next hour, Claudia looked over Zoë's assignments and tried to get a handle on how far behind Zoë was. It was overwhelming. No wonder Zoë hardly tried any more. She tried to pin down one or two small tasks that Zoë could take care of that evening without help. But when she finally got up from the table to get ready for Andi's party, she understood Zoë's feeling of hopelessness.

"You work on these two assignments this evening, and tomorrow we'll handle the rest, okay?"

Zoë sighed heavily again. "I'll try."

* * *

Andi's apartment was in a small building in a pleasant wooded area on the outskirts of the city. When Claudia pulled into the parking lot beside the building, she noticed that there were already quite a few cars in the guest spaces, and wondered how many of those people would be at Andi's party. She felt a momentary apprehension at the thought of being in a crowded noisy space with strangers all evening, but she had promised Andi she would come, and she really did need a change of scenery tonight.

Andi greeted her at the door and Claudia was ushered into the small but delightful apartment. There were already numerous people there, but looking around, Claudia saw only open, friendly faces, and instead of wild noise, there were several quiet conversations going on in different corners. At the dining table, there was some kind of card game going on. When Andi showed her the deck out the back door of the kitchen, she saw that Naomi had already arrived and was deep in thoughtful conversation with a nicely dressed, earnest young man.

"They look like they're getting along just fine," Claudia whispered to Andi, as Andi pointed out the snacks and beverages. Claudia set her bowl of guacamole on the counter alongside the other goodies, and poured herself a glass of white wine.

"Yes, I invited Ted on purpose for Naomi's sake. I knew they were perfect for each other." Andi picked up a chocolate chip cookie and took a big bite out of it. "He's a mathematics instructor at the college, and I think he's a darling. I helped him with his bathroom project. He's got the nicest little starter home in Cherry Valley." She finished the cookie and licked her fingers. "He's single but he put a bidet in his master bathroom. I think he's planning to be a thoughtful husband." She smiled mischievously.

Claudia laughed and then shushed her when she saw the door to the deck open and Naomi and her new friend walk in, still concentrating on their discussion.

"Would you like some wine?" Claudia offered as they approached.

Naomi looked up at Ted, who came over to look at the bottles on the counter. After some discussion, Ted poured a couple of glasses of wine for them both, and then they wandered off to watch the card game in the dining room.

Claudia looked at Andi who was grinning widely, and nudged her with her elbow. "Yes, you get all the credit. I'll let you be the maid of honor." When she turned around though, Andi's attention was on the front door. Claudia followed her gaze and blushed to see that Jeff had arrived.

"May I have credit for this too?" Andi whispered, giving Claudia a little push toward the door. "I think I'll be buying several new dresses in the near future."

Claudia allowed herself to be propelled through the crowd to where Jeff was standing, exchanging greetings with others in the room.

"Hurry, Claudia, that's Randy Candy. I think she's slept with everyone in the room, and is starting on her second round. She seems to have her eye on Jeff tonight."

Claudia sped up and reached Jeff just as Candy slid her hand into his, gazing into his eyes and laughing. Claudia came to a halt, and Jeff looked up, obviously embarrassed.

"Claudia, there you are," Jeff said with relief. He placed Candy's hand in Claudia's, "Candy, have you met my friend Claudia Gilmore?" Behind Candy's back, he mouthed the words *Help me!*

The two women looked at Jeff, Claudia, with an expression of amusement, Candy, irritation.

"It's so good to meet you, Candy." Claudia said, pumping the other woman's hand vigorously. "Come with me while I get another glass of wine and you can tell me all about yourself."

"Uh, sure," Candy said reluctantly allowing herself to be led to the kitchen.

As Claudia poured herself another glass of wine, she tried to maintain a conversation with Candy, while surreptitiously keeping an eye on Jeff's attempts to stay on the other side of the room. Finally, she decided she had done her bit, and she allowed Candy to wander away in search of a more stimulating group to hang with.

"Whew," Claudia turned around and saw Jeff slip around the crowd to stand beside her.

"Sorry to do that to you," he said. "I have to be more and more creative in getting away from her at parties. Thanks for helping out."

"No problem."

"Would you like to escape the crunch here? We could go outside for some fresh air."

"I would love that." Claudia tucked her hand in Jeff's and they made their way out the front door again.

"So," Jeff said as he led her down a path behind the building. "We didn't really talk a lot this morning. How is everything going?"

Claudia glanced over at Jeff's warm gaze and hesitated. She needed to confide in him about her dilemma. Jeff was dependable and wise, and even better, was here, showing an interest in her and her feelings.

"What is it? Is something wrong?"

"Actually, I have a problem, and I'd really like your advice."

"Tell me." They found a bench along the walk and sat down. Claudia clasped her hands together. Jeff sat patiently while she gathered her thoughts.

Her words came slowly at first, then faster and faster. She explained about the work she had been doing while she was a student, how much she loved it and how much respect her professor had given her. She described the phone call from her father, ordering her home.

"What did he say? He must have had some kind of reason."

"He implied that he couldn't afford it. But now here's what happened just the other day." She went on to tell about the exciting news from Dr. Spencer and the reactions she got from everyone in her family.

"I thought they'd be proud. I thought they'd be happy for me. If my dad couldn't afford to send me to graduate school, he should be glad that I have a guaranteed stipend. It shouldn't cost him a thing. But he refuses to change his mind. He just says I can't go."

"How did you leave it with your professor?"

"I told her I was coming."

"Is that what you really want?"

"I...I do. I hate my job, Jeff. I'm not meant to be someone's secretary typing papers about things that don't interest me. I had been writing my own papers, don't you see? Papers that represented my own work—work that I did myself—that I could even publish if I just went back there and kept at it."

"I do understand. I'm not a researcher, like you, but I know what it's like to be proud of the work you do—when you're good at something."

"I'm sure you do."

"You want to know what I think?"

"Yes. I do."

"You should go."

"I know I should."

"What's wrong then? He can't really stop you, you know. What can he do to you?"

Claudia had no answer to that.

"I don't know. I think I'm afraid. I have been all my life."

"Well, he's a scary guy."

Claudia chuckled at that.

"But you're all grown up now. You should run your own life, especially since you don't need him to pay your way anymore."

"You're right. I *am* grown up. But sometimes I am not very gutsy. Maybe I'll just sneak out in the dead of night some time."

"Ha. No. Walk out with everyone watching. Be strong."

"Hmm. I'll think about it. But, I do think I'm going to go."

"And when would you leave?"

"Quite soon actually. She wants me in just a few weeks. But—I'm not eager to leave *you*, you know."

Jeff looked at Claudia, his expression unreadable. "But, you do have to decide what's important, right? And what's not."

Claudia was bewildered. "Wait, that's not the way I would put it. Is that what you think? You aren't important to me? Or are you telling me that I'm not important to you?"

"Look, it's okay. It's not even like we've been together very long. This time, anyway."

Claudia was dismayed at the direction this conversation was going. She really did want this time to be different. She didn't quite know how to make it all come out right; feelings were just too complicated all around. She reached out and put her hand on Jeff's arm.

"Jeff ..."

For a moment, Jeff looked as though he would shake her hand off and turn away from her. But then, he seemed to make a decision and his expression softened. He glanced quickly around and then pulled Claudia into his arms. Before she knew it, Jeff was kissing her: on her neck, on her cheeks, her closed eyes, her mouth.

Claudia sank into his embrace wholeheartedly. She reached her hand up and grasped the back of his head. She closed her eyes and the rest of the world disappeared as Jeff ran his hands down her shoulders and behind her back to hold her close. By the time he drew back to look at her, she was feeling a little dizzy and had to grab his shoulder so that she could recover. She wiped her eyes and laughed shyly. He pulled her up to her feet before taking her hand again and continuing their walk.

"So, you told this professor you would come."

"I told her that I want to. She's sending me the paperwork now." She looked at Jeff apologetically. "You do understand don't you, Jeff? I can't be a secretary in my father's law firm for the rest of my life. I need to do something I'm good at!"

"Of course I understand that. I'm just sorry we have to say goodbye again."

"Jeff?" Claudia asked hesitantly, "Do we really have to say good-bye?"

Jeff's eyes flashed with anger. "You never did say goodbye last time. You could skip that part again this time too."

Claudia felt wounded. She turned back toward Andi's apartment, stumbling a little in the dark. As she regained her balance, she mumbled, "That's not exactly what I meant."

Jeff was instantly contrite. "I'm sorry, Claudia. I just don't want to lose you again."

"I don't either. I don't think we should have to."

Jeff took Claudia's hand and pulling her into his arms, he kissed her again, gently and lingeringly. She wanted that moment to last forever, but finally they parted and moved to rejoin the party. She hoped that no one could tell she had just been kissed soundly, but it turned out that she had nothing to worry about. The card game at the dining room table was holding the interest of more than just those who were playing. Apparently, that particular card game required a lot of advice and cheering from an audience, because she heard numerous calls like, "Throw two down!" and "Hold right there!" and then friendly laughter.

When the game had finished, and the participants all rose to refill their drinks, Claudia found herself being pulled away from her place beside Jeff by Naomi and her new friend, Ted, who had the deck of cards in his hand.

"Hey," Ted said, "I hear you play a mean game of cribbage."

Claudia laughed. "Sure do. Naomi and I used to spend our Saturday nights racking up the games, while our more popular classmates were out living the wild life."

Ted pointed at the pile of games in the corner. "Andi was prepared for the two of you, it seems."

Claudia and Naomi settled in and Naomi set up pegs while Claudia shuffled the deck. Before long, the same crowd that so enthusiastically cheered on the poker players had gathered, and were watching their cribbage game. "Throw the ones!" "Play your queen!" even when neither of them had queens. The others just seemed to love getting into the action.

Though she felt like her business with Jeff was not finished, Claudia was beginning to relax. These people were such genuinely friendly folks. Here was Andi, bouncing around offering people drinks, and bringing cookies to the card players, so they didn't have to get up from their all-important match. Andi came over to introduce her boyfriend, Stewart, who also appeared to know Jeff pretty well. The two men talked about their work together on a home in a new development going up on the outskirts of town. Andi and Stewart seemed to really enjoy each other. Every time Andi walked past Stewart, he would reach out and touch her, and she would smile or hold his hand for just a moment. Then he would let her go, and she would be off to open another bottle of wine or bring a plate of chips for her friends to snack on.

Jeff sat beside Claudia watching for a while, but then he moved off to have an energetic conversation with someone Claudia thought looked familiar but couldn't quite place. In fact, she felt that way about several of the others at the party. She felt awkward thinking that she should know their names but didn't. She had forgotten to ask Andi to subtly remind her of the others' identities, especially if they were people who were likely to know Claudia from school or from anywhere else. She was glad to have the cribbage game to focus on, so that she could try to absorb the conversations around her without actively participating.

At the end of the evening, Claudia was happier than she'd been in a long time. Andi and her friends were comfortable people to be around. They made no demands on her, nor did they watch her carefully for inadvertent mistakes or faults. There was just a genuine sense of camaraderie and fun. She was beginning to feel glad to be home, even if only for a while.

CHAPTER 13

Sunday morning Claudia needed the alarm to wake up. She had gotten home from Andi's party by midnight, but had lain in bed reviewing the evening in her head—all the conversations of the evening and the moment in the darkness when Jeff had held her close. Now she reached for the alarm clock and turned it off. She was still groggy and had a pain behind her eyes, but she was happy.

A door slammed elsewhere in the house, and she could hear footsteps in the hallway. "Claudia." Her mother was at the door. "Where is Zoë?"

"I don't know. She's not in her room?"

"No." Her mother looked worried. "I don't think she's been home at all since yesterday. Her bed doesn't look slept in." Then she shrugged, and the worried expression turned into impatience. "Well, it's almost time to go to church. Get up."

"I'm coming," she answered, leaping out of the bed. She grabbed a dress out of the closet and rushed into the bathroom to take a quick shower. Brushing her teeth, she realized that there wouldn't be time for her to eat breakfast. She could only hope that her stomach wouldn't growl during the sermon.

Claudia and Benjamin both ran out the door at the same time, just as the car was being backed out of the garage. Sitting in the back seat, they smiled secretively at each other behind their parents' backs. She felt like she was a child again. Her mother was inspecting her hairdo in the mirror in the front seat, and her father had two hands on the wheel, left on the ten, and right on the two, just as he always did.

"Roger darling, I'll have to meet with the Ladies' Guild following the service, for just a few minutes. You need to help the ushers count the offering this morning, don't forget."

"I remember," he scowled. "I never forget my obligations." He turned in his seat to include Claudia and Benjamin. "I expect the two of you to find something useful to do too. Don't just look for your friends to hang around with."

Claudia sighed imperceptibly and gazed out the window. When they finally arrived at the church, she squared her shoulders and waded into the crowd, smiling and greeting people, just as if she had never been gone. She sat demurely beside her mother through the service—her eyes on the minister, watching him go through his paces. She knew the drill. She stood at the right times, sat down when the others did with her knees together, leaning slightly to the side, just like a lady should. During the sermon, she nodded and smiled when Pastor Lindberg told his story about the sinner who came back to the fold. She looked serious when he railed about temptation, and she shook her head in anguish when he spoke of those who succumbed and needed God's help.

As a child, Claudia had perfected the skill of seeing through her lashes, while appearing to have her eyes closed. During the prayer following the sermon, Claudia sneaked a peek at the people around her. Her mother had her head bowed and her eyes closed tightly. She held Claudia's hand on one side, and her husband's on the other. Her father, on the other hand, did not bow his head. His back was strong and straight and his head was held high. Instead of directing his attention inward, as in prayer, he was staring intently into the distance. Claudia followed his gaze.

Down the same row, but across the aisle, a strikingly beautiful woman, who looked to be in her thirties, was also holding hands with the people on both sides, but was looking directly back at Claudia's father, boldly signaling with her green flashing eyes, and mouthing words with her lips. Claudia thought she understood the words "my house" before the woman's green eyes met with Claudia's blue ones.

Instead of showing embarrassment, the woman stared with hostility for a second or two, before turning back to Claudia's father, setting her chin, and then lowering her face in mock prayer. Claudia suddenly realized that her own eyes were wide open, so that when she looked back at her father, their eyes met. Claudia's face registered surprise and confusion, her father's sudden shock and embarrassment, and then anger and a warning. She heard the pastor intone, "In Jesus' name we pray." The congregation replied, "Amen."

Throughout the rest of the service, Claudia went through the motions but didn't try to comprehend anything. She couldn't help but watch the woman down the aisle. She was quite lovely, her black wavy hair tied neatly back in a bun with tendrils hanging loose around the edges. Her fine-featured face had a classic chin and well-defined cheekbones. She looked like she was wearing makeup but obviously didn't need much. Her figure was perfect with generous curves in all the right places and the lack of embellishments on her simply cut dress made it that much more stunning. The man next to her in the pew must have been her husband. He touched her knee with a proprietary air and handed over her purse, which she then searched for an envelope to put in the offering plate. She seemed to be aware of Claudia's interest but didn't look her way.

After the final hymn, Claudia rose and followed her family down the aisle, shaking hands and greeting others until they reached the narthex. Then her father headed off to the office to count money, her mother went to the basement to have her meeting, and Claudia was left to cool her heels with Benjamin.

"Benjamin, did you notice anything funny going on during church today?" Claudia queried hesitantly.

He looked at her in surprise. "No, nothing more funny than usual. What do you mean?"

She paused, then blurted out, "Dad was making eyes at some woman across the aisle."

Benjamin took a deep breath. "I was hoping you wouldn't notice. He's usually much less blatant than he was today."

"Usually?"

"Yeah. He and Mom have this unspoken agreement that if she doesn't have to know about it, he can do whatever he wants."

"Yuck."

"Yeah."

"So, he really is seeing that woman? This is making me sick."

"Well, don't say anything to Mom and Dad. Here they come."

Claudia frowned in consternation while her mother and father rejoined them. The family headed toward the Cadillac in the front row of the parking lot. After stopping a few more times for her mother to compliment a hairdo or exchange information about the next guild meeting, they were in the car and backing out of their space.

❋ ❋ ❋

Jeff had been planning to sleep in that Sunday, but the telephone had rung early with a frantic customer pleading for help. He was a sucker for a compliment, so he showered, grabbed his tools, and headed over to the country club to see what the problem was and earn a few extra dollars.

Just as he thought, the wiring that he had warned the club about over the Christmas holidays had finally shorted out. He was going to have to work extra fast so that the club could serve brunch by eleven.

As he was wrapping up his patch with electrical tape, he looked up to see the manager's assistant, Tyler, poke his worried face around the door.

"Jeff, Miss Arthur sent me down to ask you how you're doing. They're going to need to be able to turn on lights and open the door in a half hour."

Jeff stuffed the box back into the wall. "I can turn the electricity on in about ten minutes, but the job won't be done. I told your boss months ago, it will take longer than a couple of hours to make things right. I'm going to need to build a second box with at least four new circuits and rearrange things so you aren't overloading the one in the kitchen any more. Why don't you ask her when she's going to have me come out and finish the job?"

"I'll mention it to her. But you know she doesn't take too well to being told what to do."

"If I'm ever going to be able to do it right, I'm going to need six hours with the power down. Until you give me that block of time, you'll continue to have occasional outages like this one."

"Well, write it all up, and I'll make sure she sees it. That's the best I can do."

"I'll put it on the invoice. It's the only way I can cover myself, so she can't sue me when this happens again." As he spoke, Jeff popped a power screwdriver around the four corner screws of the cover plate to the overtaxed junction box, and began gathering his tools back into his bag. Finally, he switched on the power. "I'm going to sit in the office to do the paperwork. You tell Miss Arthur she can fire up the warming trays."

✳ ✳ ✳

Roger Gilmore stopped the car at the door to the country club and handed the key to the valet. Claudia was secretly amused to be helped out of the car by the doorman, but she smiled politely and followed her mother through the door and into the dining room. Her mother immediately started greeting all her high-society friends left and right, many of whom noticed Claudia and wanted to include her in their conversations. Claudia did her best to remember who they all were, but it had been a long time since she'd been home. She had to resort to the strategy of making vague exclamations of fake recognition without ever actually addressing people directly by name or referring to any specific event or occurrence in the past. It was exhausting. Claudia was relieved when her mother, realizing what trouble she was in, finally told her to go choose a table for the family and to let the servers know they were there.

The table she found for them was in an ideal position. They would be able to see the whole room, including the buffet and everybody standing in its line. She knew her parents liked scanning the crowd, so when the rest of the family joined her, she and Benjamin sat with their backs to the room and let their parents have the seats against the wall. For that reason, she did not see who was behind her until she felt a hand on her shoulder and saw her father's huge, satisfied smile.

"Nathan," he exclaimed. "Come sit down." He looked around the table and gave a brief explanation. "Nathan is here alone so I offered him a place at our table." Turning to his wife, he said, "Annette, have you met Nathan, Anthony Emerson's son?"

"No, I don't think I have." She smiled politely.

"And this is our eldest, Benjamin." The two young men shook hands.

"Nathan is one of our up-and-coming young lawyers. He's also Claudia's boss."

"Thank you for the compliment, Mr. Gilmore."

"It's very nice to meet you, Nathan." Claudia's mother quickly took charge of the situation. "I'm so glad you're joining us. Claudia, isn't this nice?"

Claudia tried to smile but was feeling decidedly unnatural.

"I'd be happy to join you, Mr. and Mrs. Gilmore." And turning to Claudia, "Would that be all right with you?"

Claudia, hiding her dismay, moved to jump out of her chair. "Of course, Nathan, that would be nice. Yes...nice. Umm, I'll find you a chair."

Nathan pushed her down on her chair and smiled. "No, that won't be necessary." He snapped his fingers, and a waiter appeared with an extra chair and place setting. Claudia moved to the side so Nathan could join them.

The three men immediately launched into an involved discussion about economics and the political situation in Washington. Claudia's mother played the hostess, passing butter, asking for the salt, pouring wine, and smiling for the nonexistent cameras. Claudia sat quietly, her head turning left and right, as though she were at a tennis match, waiting for the end of their lunch so she could escape to her book again, or at least go where she did not feel obliged to pretend to admire the sheer genius of the intellectual giants who surrounded her.

She was surprised at her own cynicism. After all, lunches at the club had been a regular occurrence throughout her youth. Why should she suddenly feel so intolerant of them?

*** * ***

Jeff had to slip through the dining room to leave the invoice in the manager's office on the other side of the building. He knew he wasn't dressed for the country club scene himself, but it was fun to watch the patrons in their Sunday best, sitting and posing and trying to impress each other. As his eyes scanned across the room, he couldn't help but notice Claudia's parents seated at a table across the room. That must be Claudia with her back to him, but who was that sitting next to her?

At that exact moment, the man next to Claudia who had been talking enthusiastically with his hands, laid one on her shoulder, and the other on her hand. Jeff could not see Claudia's face, but it looked to him that she was gazing up at her neighbor adoringly. Then she broke her glance and twisted around to look out into the room. Her eyes met Jeff's. Her face went through a range of emotions, which he wasn't quite certain how to interpret. He frowned and looked at her questioningly.

CHAPTER 14

Claudia felt a jolt of pleasure at the sight of Jeff across the room. Dressed in his coveralls and carrying a large pack of tools he looked so comfortably unengaged with all the connecting and networking. A new awareness washed over her as she glanced back at the group sitting around her own table. Without realizing that she was interrupting a story she was supposed to be fascinated by, she quickly grabbed her purse and said, "I'm sorry. I'll be right back." She was gone before anyone could protest.

Jeff's frown turned into a smile of pleasure as she approached.

"So, who's the octopus?"

She dragged him around the corner so they could talk in relative privacy. "He's my boss." She made a wry face. "I was trapped there for a while."

Jeff rolled his eyes. "You were enjoying it. I could tell."

Claudia sputtered, "How can you know anything? You were only looking at my back! Besides, we're in a public place and I'm trying to be pleasant!"

"So, for everybody's peace of mind, you'll just let this guy put his hands all over you like he owns you?"

"Jeff, I thought I was glad to see you. Now I'm not so sure. Here I have my father trying to run my life, and now you say my boss is acting like he owns me. Well, I don't see that you're behaving any different!"

"Wait a minute. I thought you were going to quit that job? Why are you still trying to impress your boss?"

Claudia didn't have an answer for that. She didn't really know why she still felt like she had to please Nathan and her father, and that fact had her almost in tears from anger. "I don't know! But it's my business, not yours. You tell me I should run my own life, but if I don't do it your way or to your timetable, you criticize me! You don't own me either!" She put her fists on her hips. "I think I am going to go finish my meal. Maybe I'll see you later!" She turned her back on Jeff and marched back into the dining room. Before she had gotten halfway to their table though, Claudia decided she'd better go to the powder room and see what her face looked like.

As she was standing in front of the mirror angrily brushing her hair, her mother joined her and began to renew her lipstick.

"Your father thinks a lot of that young man."

Claudia turned to look at her mother. "Which young man are you talking about, Mom?"

"Why, Nathan, of course!"

"Of course Dad likes him, Mom. Nathan's a younger version of Dad." She put her brush back in her bag, and withdrew a nail clipper, just for something else to do. "What do you think of him?"

"Well, he'd be quite a catch for you, of course. He's clearly got a good career ahead of him."

"A catch for me? I don't know that I want to even think about that. Mom, you don't know anything about him as a person. What do you suppose he is really like?"

"What a silly question, Claudia." Her mother averted her eyes and dug into her own purse, pulling out a mascara, which she began to apply to her eyelashes.

"Why is that so silly?" Claudia could not let it go. She did not know why, but she really felt like she wanted some motherly advice. "Mom?"

"Claudia, he comes from a very upright family," her mother said emphatically. She nodded her head to herself in the mirror. "His parents are good people. They gave a large donation to the Mozart Society last year. In fact, I think they are now lifetime members.

And his father has kept your own father quite busy with some very profitable clients. I'm sure you and Nathan would make a lovely couple."

Claudia looked at her mother in amazement. "Mom, you haven't said a word about Nathan himself, just his family and his standing in society. What do you think about him?"

"Well, he seems quite intelligent. Your father said that he graduated high in his class at Northwestern. We're both very impressed by him. Why shouldn't we be?"

"Mom, I just wonder about him. He's pretty sure of himself. I can tell what kind of person he is, because he talks up a good line. But I don't think he knows me at all. He hasn't shown any interest in hearing anything I have to say."

"Darling, that's how men are. He's trying to impress you. You'll get your turn to talk later."

"But…"

"It's nice when a man notices you." Claudia's mother pushed her mascara back into her purse and snapped it closed. "He could probably have any young woman he wanted. We should go back in there. You don't want him to lose interest, do you?"

"I'm not sure I care." Claudia muttered as she followed her mother back to the table. As she smiled politely into the gaze of her fiery-eyed young boss, in his sharp expensive Armani suit, she couldn't help but think of the muscular, but gentle, electrician that she had left on the other side of the room.

✳ ✳ ✳

Jeff's thoughts were in a turmoil as he drove home as fast as he could. He had only seen Claudia a couple of times now, but he felt consumed by murderous rage at the slick lawyer who got to see her every day, and was so confident of himself that he could grab her like that, right there, at the table with her parents. How could he be so jealous? They had only had a couple of dates, for Pete's sake.

He screeched to a halt in the driveway and, leaving his tools in the van, strode into the house and slammed the door. For a while, he just paced, unable to decide what to do first or whether he wanted to just go back to bed. Knowing he would never get back to sleep now, he finally went into the kitchen to start a pot of coffee brewing. While he waited for the coffee, he showered and washed his hair. By the time he was dressed in a clean pair of jeans, the smell of the rich dark roast was wafting through the house and he was feeling a little better.

He forced himself to sit down and read the newspaper while he drank his coffee. Then he went down to the basement to lift weights. He pushed himself hard all afternoon, figuring that all that anger and frustration might as well accomplish something worthwhile. Doing extra reps, and several sets instead of just one or two made him really sweat. So much, in fact, that he needed another shower at the end of his workout. But finally he felt like he was calming down.

He was just combing his wet hair when he heard a banging on the door and Stewart's voice calling his name.

Jeff opened the door, and Stewart shoved his way in carrying a case of Budweiser, and a bag of pretzels. "You up for some poker? The guys are all on their way over."

"You're kidding!" Jeff looked outside. No one yet, so he shut the door. "Are you serious? Tell me you're joking so I don't have to shut off the lights and hide down in the basement for the next hour."

"Hey man! I don't joke about serious things like beer and poker. Rob called me, and Arnie called him, and Tony wanted in on the deal too. My house is a mess, so I told them all to come to yours." He looked around at the tidy living room. "Yours looks great. Let's go get the folding chairs and the cards and poker chips." Stewart looked innocently at Jeff, who was still standing there, staring at him in disbelief.

"Wow, you have nerve!" Jeff glanced out the window to the street one more time. Turning back to Stewart, considering whether he should throw him out the door headfirst, he finally laughed and shook his head. "You are so lucky that I need a distraction today." He took the case of beer from him, and headed into the kitchen to put the bottles in the refrigerator so they could chill. He pulled out some snacks, opened a couple of his cheaper bottles of wine, and set some glasses on the counter.

✳ ✳ ✳

Jeff served himself some cheese and crackers and sat down to the game. For a while, he just listened to the banter without joining in. He didn't really want to tell his poker buddies what was going on in his life. He didn't understand it himself, how could he explain it to his friends?

"Hey, you know, I managed to get hold of two tickets to the Cubs game on Friday," Arnie began. "Who wants to cover the gas for the trip in?"

"Wow, I'd really like to, but Barbie's sister is coming to visit from Tennessee." Tony studied his cards. "We're going to have a huge houseful of folks for a while. Jenny has three kids, ages three to six. I think I'm going to have to move in with you, Jeff."

Jeff threw a couple of chips into the center. "Yeah right, Tony."

"Yeah, I'm going to go home and pack up as soon as I'm done with this hand." Tony arranged his cards a couple of ways and finally threw his cards down in mock disgust. "Oh well, I'll wait until after the next hand."

Rob tossed a couple more chips on the table and asked for another card. "Well, I'm free Friday."

"That's great, Rob. We'll leave right after work." Arnie looked at Jeff. "Hey, dude. I could get another ticket if you want to go too."

"No, that's all right. I'll probably be busy anyway."

"Yeah, what with?"

Stewart's eyes twinkled as he said, "Jeff's girlfriend's back in town."

"Whoa," Rob raised his eyebrows in curiosity. "Why haven't I heard anything about this?"

Jeff scowled as he studied his own cards. "There's not much to tell. We used to date, then she went away to college, and now she's home living with her family again. For now anyway."

"So are you guys back together?"

"Well, I sure can't get her off my mind. But she has a lot going on."

Stewart's interest was piqued. "What do you mean? I thought you were doing well at the party last night."

"Yeah, but today I was at the country club doing a job, and who did I see but Claudia, sitting with her family and some hot shot guy who was sitting way too close to her. Her parents looked like they were pretty impressed by him, I could tell."

Stewart narrowed his eyes. "Hmmm, but what I want to know is, was Claudia?"

"I don't think so. She said she would have liked to get away." Jeff threw down another swallow of his lager. "But, she didn't seem to be trying to discourage him very much either, from what I could see. He was a real country club sort—starched shirt, thousand dollar suit, styled hair."

Rob grimaced at the image. "Well, if that's what she's into, she's probably a real fake herself, and you're better off without her."

Stewart laughed. "That won't work with Jeff, Rob. I already tried it on him, and he leaped to her defense." Then he turned to Jeff, "Looks like you've got some competition, buddy. You're going to have to work a little harder—and faster."

"I don't know how I can work any faster than I already am." Jeff grumbled. "I took her out for dinner once, saw her again yesterday morning, and then last night at Andi's party. I woke up this morning and went to the club to fix a short, and there they were."

"Well OK," Stewart said, "Let's make a plan of action for Jeff, guys. He obviously needs our help."

Tony, being the only one among them who had successfully managed to date and then marry a woman, furrowed his brow in concentration. "Well, you need to take her out to dinner."

"I've already done that!" Jeff protested.

"All right, all right, I'm just getting rolling here. Get me another beer while I think."

Jeff obligingly got up for him and brought back a Miller. Tony cracked it open and took a long swallow.

"Stewart poked him in the belly, "You're stalling."

"No, I was thirsty."

"Tell Jeff how you won your lady love."

"You're going to laugh."

"No, we won't. Will we guys?"

"No, certainly not."

"Of course not."

"I promise."

"Jeff needs your wisdom. We all need your wisdom."

Tony looked from one to the other. "Well, I called her at night to tell her goodnight. And then I called her in the morning to tell her good morning."

"Hmm. That's a little creepy. That's like stalking."

"No it's not. It's all to let her know that you're thinking of her all the time."

Stewart pulled a greasy pad of paper and a pencil out of his back pocket and started writing. He muttered as he wrote, "Call her on the phone to tell her all sorts of trivial things." Then he looked up, "Keep going."

Tony smiled, a faraway look in his eyes. "Send her a card in the middle of the week, for no special reason. Then you have to start giving her little presents. Then she'll have stuff lying around to remind her of you."

"What kind of stuff? I need some examples."

"Something she likes. So you can convince her you've been paying attention all this time."

"Well, what did you give Barbie?"

"I gave her some flowers once, and some chocolates another time. Then I gave her a chess set."

"A chess set?" Jeff scratched his head.

"It's so we have something to do when we're alone together."

"I could think of something better than chess." Stewart leered.

"No." Tony spoke patiently. "You have to prove that you have more than one thing on your mind. Idiot."

"…more than one thing on your mind…" Stewart's pen scratched against the paper.

"I get it." Jeff said. He grabbed the paper from under Stewart's hand and stuffed it into his pocket. He was getting irritated again.

Rob was listening and shuffling the cards over and over again. "Are we going to play poker here?"

* * *

"Mom?" Claudia found her mother sitting at her desk.

"Yes, Claudia?"

"I wanted to talk to you about what happened earlier today. I'm confused."

"What happened? What do you mean?"

"You know, when we were at the club, and Nathan came to eat with us. I was under the impression that Dad had planned the whole thing and that he somehow wants to see me and Nathan be together."

"Would that be so bad? Nathan is just the sort of man your father would love to have as a son-in-law. He's from such a good family. And he would bring you a great deal of prestige."

"But, what about me? Doesn't it matter what I think of him? And shouldn't there be love?"

"Yes, of course. That's very important, dear. But, love will come when everything else is right. And since marriage involves more than just the bride and the groom, a young man who is interested in you should know that he needs to win over the entire family, and the father most of all. Your father needs to be happy with whomever you choose as your partner in life."

"Mom!" Claudia cried in alarm. "I haven't chosen a partner yet. Please don't say things like this to Nathan. I have to work for him! He's going to think I'm after him!"

"Of course I'm not talking like this to him. But it's important that you know how to play the game yourself! It's a serious competition and you need to know the rules—and the strategy!"

Claudia had never seen this side of her mother. Love, a game? A competition? Strategy? She knew that some of the girls she knew at school thought this way, but her mother? This whole thing was making her uncomfortable.

"What is the strategy here? How do you think I'm supposed to play this game?"

Her mother's smile was almost coquettish. "That's the fun part." She looked at her watch and jumped. "Oh no, I have to get dinner. We can talk about this tonight."

She ran into the kitchen. Claudia looked after her for a moment. Then she headed up the stairs to start a load of laundry.

Dinner was quiet. Zoë still hadn't shown up, and she hadn't been in her room when Claudia checked earlier. Claudia had sent her numerous text messages, but Zoë hadn't replied to any of them. Claudia was worried. Where could she be? She felt a pang of guilt, thinking about how she had promised to help her with her studies today. But, she was secretly relieved that she didn't have to spend the whole evening on high school homework. It was a time of her life she didn't mind leaving behind. She hadn't been very interested in most of the classes she had taken, but they were required for graduation. Much of the time was spent on what she thought of as busy work. It wasn't surprising to her that Zoë was floundering. Her sister was not the sort of person who could buckle down and do things she didn't want to do for some nebulous far-in-the-future goal. If it wasn't something she chose, and she couldn't see a purpose for it, she wouldn't be able to force herself to do it. Claudia did remember that she'd had some exceptional teachers, and she hoped that Zoë got to take classes with them. They had actually made her high school years worthwhile. It might be worth going over Zoë's schedule with her to try to fit some of those classes in next year.

Claudia stuck her head into her mother's room to see if she was free. She was changing the sheets on the bed.

"Your father has gone back to the office to get some business done. He won't be home until late. He works so hard."

Claudia had her doubts, given what she had seen at church that morning. She looked sharply at her mother, wondering how much she knew or if she was truly as unaware as she seemed to be.

"What?" her mother asked, her firm, determined tone discouraging comment.

"Uh, nothing." Claudia decided that she would put off this talk until she had figured out how to say what she wanted to say. "Mom? I'm worried about Zoë. I haven't seen her all day, and she and I were going to go over her schoolwork together this afternoon."

Concern flashed across her mother's face to be replaced by irritation. "I'm sure she's fine. She will probably come waltzing in long after dinnertime, never telling us what she did or where she was."

"You think so?"

"That's what usually happens," her mother sighed.

"I hope so." Claudia couldn't help but frown though. What if something were seriously wrong? Shouldn't they be out looking for Zoë? She leaned against the doorjamb, brooding.

"Don't worry! Everything will be all right." Claudia's mother pulled up the bedspread a little too firmly and then patted it into place. "We were going to have a talk about men, weren't we?"

"You're talking about our conversation earlier." Claudia tried to be cheerful. "Well, if you want to teach me all your secrets, I wouldn't mind. It certainly couldn't hurt."

"Well, I wouldn't give them all away. A woman has to keep some secrets to herself, even from her daughter." She raised her eyebrows suggestively.

"You're talking about the game, right?"

"Of course, dear. That is something that must be passed down from mother to daughter, and I think it is time for you to learn."

"Well, then go ahead."

"The main thing you have to learn is timing. In the beginning of a relationship, you want to stress certain things, so that you will proceed to the next stage. At this point, you want to be attractive and also just hint at more to come. Don't give too much at first though, or there will be nothing left for him to look forward to, and he will go on to other conquests."

"Mom, you're being rather vague. What do you mean?"

"Goodness, Claudia. Do I have to spell it out?" Her mother looked uncomfortable. "What I mean, is that in the early days, you just don't give too much of yourself away."

"Mom, are you talking about sex?"

"Well, of course. But not just that. There are those private parts of yourself that you shouldn't share too much of. Men don't always want to be burdened with your problems or your emotions. They have enough to deal with, just doing their jobs and getting ahead. Sometimes it's just better to keep those things to yourself."

Claudia knew that her mother was talking from her own experience. But, how sad that she had to justify her husband's insensitivity to herself like that. And how completely she had to hide her feelings. She always presented herself as though nothing was ever wrong and she was never upset about anything. Claudia was just now beginning to see bits and pieces of real feeling behind that perfect façade. She knew her mother never let it show when her father was present.

"Hmm, I've never thought of it that way, Mom."

"I could tell, darling." her mother said indulgently. That's why I thought it was time to give you lessons."

"Okay. Anything else?"

"Touch is a very special commodity. Don't let him touch you too much at this stage. You need to keep him wanting more, but let him know there is more there. So, you can gently brush his hand with yours while you are doing something else. That way, you keep him on edge. He'll come back over and over again, as long as you don't ever quite satisfy him."

Claudia cringed inwardly. Her mother really did treat this like a game—like she had to trick a man into wanting her. Wasn't it possible to just find someone who loved her as she was? And what would all these little tricks do to someone like Nathan, who was used to getting whatever he wanted?

"But, Mom," Claudia began to get a little nervous. "What do you do to discourage him if he wants more? I know I always feel very awkward in a situation like this, and some men are very persistent."

"Well, darling, then it's a matter of learning signals to discourage interest. Don't touch him at all, of course. That should go without saying. When you look at him, be very direct and steady. If you look down, he will see you as being a flirt. Remember Lady Di?"

Claudia learned all the secret techniques that her mother used to catch her father, and some age-old knowledge that had been passed down to her when she was Claudia's age.

It felt funny even talking about these strange little tricks. She couldn't imagine using them. It smacked of dishonesty, and Claudia wanted to believe that true love did not need such manipulations. On the other hand, it gave her a view into her parents' relationship that she had never imagined before. She could just picture her father being distant and aloof and her mother using her little wiles so that he would be intrigued by her but not know why. If her mother were to be believed, Claudia should, at every step along the way, give a little more but only hint at the next gift promised. If she played the game right, she'd be married before the year was up.

She could see Nathan Emerson being lured in by bait like this. On the other hand, she didn't want to attract him. So much about him bothered her—his certainty of his own superiority, his arrogance, his complete disinterest in Claudia's thoughts and ideas. Jeff, on the other hand, was sweet and considerate. He not only listened to her talk about her thoughts, he encouraged it. Well . . . before today when they argued at the country club. Claudia winced when she thought about how she had behaved there. She'd been so quick to jump down Jeff's throat, when he was . . . what? He was questioning her about Nathan. Jeff was jealous! She didn't need to be angry about that. It just meant that Jeff cared. Right?

Her cell phone rang and she quickly looked at the caller ID. "It's Andi, Mom. Do you mind?"

"No problem, dear. I have to get my face ready to sleep."

Chuckling at the image, Claudia pressed the phone to her ear and left the room. "Hi, Andi. What's up?"

"Have you seen your sister today?"

"Not at all. I've been so worried." Claudia whispered into the phone. "Why? Do you know something about her?"

"Do you remember I told you about those friends of hers?"

"Ye-es."

"I've seen her before with two guys, older than she is. They deal drugs. I think, anyway."

"Oh." Claudia felt sick.

"I saw those same pieces of trash just a little while ago, while I was out buying wine. I saw them in the liquor store, talking about how completely out of it Zoë was. They were laughing. You mean she's not there?"

"I haven't seen her." Claudia was feeling worse and worse. "Thanks for telling me. I better go now. I have to see if I can find her."

"Let me know if I can help."

Andi's worried voice cut off as Claudia thrust the cell phone back in her pocket and raced down the hall to Zoë's room. It was still empty, just as it had been all day. She didn't know why she expected any different. But it was pretty messy. She didn't know what she expected to see there. A sudden thought made Claudia go rushing back down the stairs and to the front hallway closet. Zoë's hiking boots and camping equipment were all gone.

Claudia walked slowly back up to her room, thinking. Zoë was saving camping equipment for a reason. She had talked with Claudia about the time they had all gone camping together and how she had been so happy there. Could she have decided to go back there alone? Claudia wondered if she would be able to find the campground again. Certainly not in the dark. Suddenly, the noise of a car pulling up broke into her thoughts and she ran, relieved, to the back door. But instead of her sister, she met her father just coming in and carrying his briefcase.

Claudia's heart fell. Her father must have seen the disappointment in her eyes, because his brow furrowed, and he asked sharply, "What?"

Claudia stammered, "Nothing, I was just, umm, getting a glass of water before going to bed. Would you like anything before I go upstairs?"

He glanced quickly toward the stairs. "No. Is your mother still awake?"

"I just left her a little while ago. She was getting ready for bed. She said you were working late. What kind of case are you working on?"

An evasive look came over his face. "Nothing you need to know about. Why?"

"I'm just curious. I find it all very interesting now that I'm working at your firm. I'd like to know more about what you do. It seems like we've never talked much about it."

"I cannot divulge my clients' secrets to you just to satisfy your idle curiosity. That would be unethical."

"I'm sorry." Claudia flushed. "I didn't mean to pry. I'll go up to my room."

She undressed slowly for bed, hoping to hear a car bringing Zoë back home. It took her a long time to fall asleep, and then she woke up groggy the next day still worried.

CHAPTER 15

Claudia could hardly focus on her work. She couldn't stop her imagination from coming up with various problems that Zoë might have encountered in the last day and a half. She had debated with herself about whether she should try again to talk with her parents or just go find Zoë herself. If Zoë was fine, then she would be worrying them needlessly, and her father would probably be furious by the time it was all over and Zoë was home safe. If Zoë was in trouble, she would be doubly so as soon as her parents learned of it, and nobody would thank Claudia for drawing their attention to it. She wished she could take the day off to go find her, but she didn't see how she could escape without telling someone at the office of her problem, and then, no doubt, her father would learn of it within the hour. No, she was just going to have to get through the day and then take off. The problem was, she didn't know her way around like she used to. And where exactly was that campsite that Zoë might have headed toward? Suddenly she had a thought and pulled out her cellphone.

"Jeff?"

"Yes, Claudia?"

"I'm so afraid for Zoë!"

Jeff didn't hesitate. "What's the matter?"

"No one has seen her since Saturday, and Andi called me last night and said that she overheard these two creepy guys in a store talking about how wasted she was. My mother isn't taking it seriously and I can't talk to my dad, so I've been waiting and worrying all this time. Please, can you go with me and help me look for her?"

"Wait just a minute." Jeff's voice was calming. "Do you know that she didn't go in to school today?"

"No." Claudia replied meekly.

"If she did go to school today, would she be home by now?"

Claudia looked at her watch. "I think so, unless she is with her friends."

"Listen. When do you get off work? Why don't you go back to your house and check to see if she's there. I'll come over and meet you there. If she's still missing, we'll go out looking. No sense in running around town if she's already made it back home on her own."

"You're probably right." Claudia was ashamed.

The decision made, Claudia settled in to watch the clock for the end of the workday.

The day turned out to be a quiet one. Nathan was busy with a case, and was barely in the office. He only came in a couple of times to rummage through the file cabinet, and then disappear again. If she had not been so distracted with worrying about Zoë, she would have wondered why Nathan was suddenly being so distant. As it was, she was relieved she didn't have to figure out how to deal with him when she had much more important things to think about. She kept herself busy all day typing up briefs and filling up the coffee machine and straightening her pencils and pens when there was nothing else to do. Once she looked up as Nathan was passing by and found him looking at her with a quizzical expression on his face. As soon as their eyes met, he spun around and strode off.

When five o'clock finally rolled around, she swept her purse up from underneath her desk and set off at a semi-run.

"Hold it!" a voice called from behind her.

She turned. "Oh, Na—," she stopped herself, "Mr. Emerson, I didn't see you there. I'm afraid I have to run today. Was there anything else you needed before I left?"

Nathan looked like he was about to say something to her, but then, to her relief, he answered, "No. I'll see you again tomorrow."

Claudia drove home as fast as she could. Just as she was pulling up the driveway, Jeff drove up to the curb in front of the house. She met him at the door to his car.

"I think I might know where she is. Do you remember when we went camping, and she came along?"

"Yes, though I think we ignored her most of the time we were there."

"Believe it or not, she had a great time and says those were the best times she's ever had."

"Hard to believe." Jeff shook his head. "She had to do everything alone. Did we even help her set up her own tent? I don't remember."

"I don't remember either." Claudia slumped against the car. "But she's been collecting camping equipment ever since, it seems. I saw a big pile of it in her closet and more of it in her room the other day. And then last night when I ransacked her room looking for some clue as to where she went, I noticed it was all gone. She seems to have packed up her big backpack and gone. She must have done it yesterday morning while we were having brunch at the country club."

The country club. Now this was awkward. Jeff looked quickly toward Claudia. She studiously looked the other way. They turned to walk into the house.

The look on her mother's face when she swung the door open to greet them made Claudia's heart sink. This was not a "Why are you bringing that boy here?" look, but a "Something horrible has happened!" look.

"What is it, Mom?" Claudia ran up the steps.

"I don't know where Zoë is! The school called and asked why she wasn't there. I couldn't find her, and I don't think she's been home since Saturday. Your father will be so angry! We have to find her." Her mother's cheeks were streaked with tears.

Claudia's guilt was crushing her. "Mom, I've been trying to figure out where she could be since yesterday, remember? Even at bedtime, I was getting worried, but Dad came home right at that same time, and he wasn't in a good mood. I was afraid. . ."

"Yes, I know. But where could she be?"

Claudia laid her hand upon her mother's shoulder. "I think I might know. I noticed she took all her camping equipment. I'm going to go check a campground that I know of. Don't worry. Jeff and I will find her."

"But what will I tell your father?" Her mother's voice was shrill.

"Mom, what's wrong with just telling him the truth? Isn't the most important thing that we find Zoë and make sure she's safe?"

"Of course, that's the most important thing! But we can't tell him about it. Believe me! That would be a disaster!"

"Okay. Calm down." Claudia slowed down her own voice. "Just tell him that Jeff and I are out on a date, and that you don't know exactly where Zoë is, but you expect her home soon. None of that is a lie. We don't have to give him a reason to be upset…yet."

"All right. All right." Her mother turned away and headed up the stairs. "I need to go fix my face. Call me as soon as you know anything."

Jeff waited until they were well on the way before he spoke, "I can't believe you are keeping important things away from your father. Don't you think he has a right to know what's going on in his own family?"

"I wish my father were someone we could go to with our problems. But, Jeff, you saw how upset my mother was just at the thought of telling my dad. I can't go against her wishes. Not right now. Besides, you know him. Imagine how he would react."

"Of course I know him. But Zoë might be in serious trouble. Don't you think he should be involved? He might be of some use to us."

"We will tell him if we have to. Until then, I would rather not have to deal with his judgment and with Zoë's disappearance at the same time. Somehow, I find that I am much more competent in dealing with stressful situations when he is not around."

"Don't you think it's time for you to learn to handle him?"

Claudia's eyes flashed. "Of course I do! I'm working on it. It's not easy, you know."

"Of course, I know that. But you aren't making much progress."

"How dare you! You have no idea what I'm doing."

"I only know what I see. And what I see is you and your mom plotting to keep your father completely in the dark for as long as you can. You won't even tell him that Zoë's been missing for almost two days. I would hate to be him—kept completely out of my own family's lives."

Claudia looked at him suddenly. Jeff looked sad.

"Jeff, you're nothing like my father and your family won't have to keep you out."

Then she changed the subject. "Do you think we should go straight to the campground? I don't know where else she would be. I've been texting her all day and she hasn't responded at all, so it makes sense that that's where she might be. I remember not being able to find much cell phone service there."

"Have you thought of calling her friends?"

"I hate to say it, but I don't actually know any of her friends. She told me that none of the smart kids will give her the time of day, so she hangs out with the freaky ones—the ones who make my parents worry about her. Andi recognized a couple of guys hanging around with Zoë recently. She says they are a bad sort, the kind who deal drugs."

"Maybe we can get hold of those guys, if Andi knows who they are. Why don't you call Andi and try to get some names. I'll head toward the campground to save time."

"Good plan." Claudia busied herself with her cell phone while Jeff drove.

Andi was able to find a couple of numbers for Claudia in the phone book, but when Claudia called them, she was unable to reach anyone. "How much further is it?" She asked.

"We're only a few minutes away. We might have to walk a ways. Because of the bird-watchers' lobbying, the road closest to the site is blocked off, but it's still available to people who don't mind hiking in. You say she has hiking shoes? How do you think she got out there?"

"Maybe she biked. I didn't notice if her bike was gone. I'm not even sure what kind of bike she has now."

"We'll see." Jeff swerved around a tight corner and headed up a narrow road that led into the woods. He had to drive along a switchback that led up higher and higher, until they finally came upon a small level area just large enough to accommodate seven or eight cars. Claudia saw one car, a real junker, sitting there already. Jeff parked the Toyota and pulled the emergency brake. He reached into his glove compartment and took out two flashlights. He handed one of them to Claudia. They both got out of the car and closed the doors, but before heading out onto the path, Jeff stood there in thought for a short while.

"What are you doing? Let's go. Which way is it?"

"Just a minute." Jeff looked around. There was nobody else in sight. Without another word, he opened the trunk and withdrew one of the handguns that they had used the other day at the firing range. He pulled out the magazine, looked at it a moment, and then pushed it back in. He checked the safety before sliding the gun into the holster and clipping it onto his tool belt.

Claudia looked at him in horror. "You think you might need a gun?"

"I hope not, but she might not be alone. And the guys with her might need to be discouraged from staying with her once we arrive. Don't mention the gun to anyone. I don't plan to take it out unless it's absolutely necessary, and I'd rather it be a surprise to the people I might have to use it on."

Claudia realized she didn't know this man any more. Jeff had become a cowboy in the time since she'd been away. On the other hand, she had to admit that at this moment she felt completely safe. They were walking down a path into the deepest part of the woods. Since the sun was also going down at the same time, the woods seemed terribly spooky. The shadows were growing, and the trees were becoming thicker, even as the undergrowth thinned. On the other hand, being there again with Jeff brought wonderful memories. When Claudia wasn't worrying about what they would find when they got to the campsite, she was beginning to remember the peaceful feeling that she got from those old woods. The air was nice and cool, and the rustling noise under their feet was soft and rhythmic.

Suddenly, Jeff held his arm out in front of Claudia to indicate that she should stop. She froze in place. Jeff signaled that he was going on ahead and she should wait. Or maybe he meant for her to stay behind him. She preferred that latter interpretation, so when he got about ten feet ahead she gave in to the temptation to follow him.

They had not gone more than twenty feet farther when Claudia heard a familiar voice. She couldn't yet understand the words, but before she could call out, Jeff again waved his hand, signaling to her to stay silent. They tiptoed forward slowly, and finally came to a small clearing containing a tent and a couple of canvas chairs. Zoë was sitting on the ground, swaying back and forth in a sensuous manner. The chairs beside the tent held two boys about Zoë's age.

All three of them seemed to be under the influence of something, Claudia couldn't tell what. But Zoë was a totally different person from the one Claudia knew her to be. She wasn't the sweet younger sister sitting on Claudia's bed exchanging confidences. Tonight she was a sleepy, sultry, sexy little femme fatale. She smiled knowingly at her companions, though what exactly she was knowing about, Claudia could only dread discovering. Claudia looked at Jeff, wondering what the plan was. Jeff wasn't moving. She would have to take charge of the situation.

Claudia stood up and strode toward her sister. Jeff reached out to grab her—too late.

"Hey Zoë, I had a heck of a time finding this place. Thanks for leaving the note though. I'm always up for a party."

Zoë looked surprised. Claudia reached her hand out to the blond on Zoë's right. "Hi! Have I met you? I'm Zoë's sister, Claudia. I just got back to town a few weeks ago." She almost didn't want to touch the creep, but she had to quickly take control of the situation. He reflexively held out his own hand though he looked like he'd rather not. Claudia pumped it energetically, then dropped it, and moved on to the other guy. He was smaller, and had his head shaved. Somehow that made him look cleaner than Mr. Golden Locks, since his hair didn't have the opportunity to stick together and hang in his eyes. But his skin was all broken out, so he seemed more like an adolescent playing tough than an evil drug dealer. She held in her laughter.

"You guys have been here since yesterday?" She spoke with a whine, trying to convey that she would have liked to have been included, rather than the dig for information that she was really interested in. "You could have waited for me!" She turned to Mr. Golden Locks and said, "So, what's good today? What's Zoë on?"

They all turned toward Zoë, who had lost her worldly air, and now just looked like her younger sister again, in the process of falling asleep. "Looks like some pretty strong stuff!"

Goldie and Razorback looked at each other, obviously unsure of how much to divulge to this new arrival. Then Goldie, who seemed to be in charge, mumbled, "She just wanted to smoke some weed tonight. But she didn't want to go to sleep, so I gave her a little cocaine too."

Zoë's voice floated dreamily over from her corner, "Don't forget. You gave me a little pink pill too. What was that?"

"A pink pill?" Claudia asked sharply, then toned it down. She glanced at Zoë quickly enough to see her lower her eyes and feign a sleepy expression. Turning to the adolescent drug dealers again, she demanded, "Were you going to hold out on me?" She knew Jeff was still crouched behind the bushes listening, and wondered if he knew what drug came in a little pink pill.

Golden boy smirked a little and winked at his friend. "It's a happy pill. You want one?" He seemed to get a little bolder.

Claudia looked at him thoughtfully. "Perhaps. But before I become hmmm, shall we say, less on top of things, why don't you give me your names and phone numbers. After all, if I like your product, I'm going to want more."

Again the two looked at each other. Then Goldie said, "You can call me Slick, and my friend here is Dude."

Claudia pouted. "You don't trust me? Does Zoë know who you are? That's not fair, you know." She tried to be convincingly sophisticated. "I had a great supplier at college, and now I don't know anyone around here. The least you could do is be a little more friendly."

"Well, if it's friendly you want." Razorback slid over to her and put his arm around her. "I can show you friendly."

Claudia tried not to gag. "You could start with your real names." She spoke in a firm voice. "And phone numbers please." She took out her own cell phone and prepared to enter their information. Just as she expected, her tone induced in them a reflexive obedience, and Razor guy began reciting numbers. She entered them into her phone, and then waited for him to give her his name.

"Tommy Parker," he mumbled. "And this is Ben Reynolds."

"You idiot!" Ben snarled at him. "You don't know we can trust her!"

Claudia had to think fast. She needed to calm these boys down, or Jeff would have to shoot them, and then there would be a mess to deal with. "Boys, boys!" She began soothingly. "Of course you can trust me. I'm Zoë's sister after all. Didn't she tell you about me? I'm going to want your product, because I have grown-up expensive taste now, after four years of living away. So, let's just get the business over with, and then we can start having fun. Is that satisfactory to you?"

Still fuming, Golden Boy—woops, Ben—folded his arms in front of his chest. "Can you pay?"

"I have a lucrative career path now. Regular income. Of course I can pay. What do you have?"

"You're going to have to make an order. I don't just carry everything with me all the time."

Zoë had been watching this interchange with something like bemusement. Claudia just hoped that Zoë wouldn't say anything to blow the momentum Claudia had going. Finally, Zoë said, "Ben, you have a whole bag of those pink pills. I saw them. And I know you have two ounces of weed. Come on, roll us a joint. My own sister deserves a taste of everything you give me."

Claudia was wondering if it was time to bring Jeff out into the open. She got up and went to the opposite site of the clearing from where she knew Jeff was. Making a show of peering into the woods, she finally said, "I wonder where Jeff is. I called and told him to come on out here. I said there was a big party going on." She turned to Ben and Tommy and said brightly, "You don't mind, do you? He was just telling me that he was wishing for some good pot, and wondered where to get it. Of course, we have to be pretty careful, because his dad is the chief of police and is always butting into our business."

Ben jumped out of his chair and hit Tommy on the shoulder. The two boys started gathering their bags together.

"We're going to have to go. Sorry, we'll have to get in touch another time." Ben said as he grabbed Tommy's arm and dragged him away. Claudia could hear him whispering angrily as they disappeared into the woods, "You better ditch that cell phone too, and get a new number. Don't you EVER talk to that chick Zoë again." His language got coarser and coarser as their voices receded into the distance.

Claudia, watching them go, suddenly began to shake. She sank down to the ground right where she was.

Claudia wondered where Jeff was now. She should have known that when she went to the other side of the clearing to draw their attention away from Jeff, they would leave in the opposite direction from where she was looking—right toward Jeff. Arrrgh. "Jeff?" she called quietly.

"Right here," he said into her ear. She jumped.

"Where have you been?"

"Watching the show." He was laughing. "You should be an actress."

Claudia laughed and trembling slightly still, pushed her hair behind her ear. "Well, I just kept thinking about you and your gun and explaining the dead bodies to the police when they came out here. That would have been a real bother and probably would have ruined our date."

"Yeah, you were great," Zoë mumbled with her eyes closed. Then she moaned. "Claudia, I'm not feeling very well." She rolled over and laid her face down on the ground.

"Oh honey," Pulling herself together, Claudia crawled over to kneel next to Zoë and stroked her hair. "What was in that pink pill anyway?"

"I don't know." Zoë wailed. "They told me it would make me happy."

"You've smoked marijuana, snorted cocaine, and swallowed a random little pink pill today? And Mom is sitting at home waiting to hear that you're still alive."

Tears rolled down Zoë's cheeks. "You can't tell her. Dad will kill me."

"Mom is worried to death about you. I have to call her and tell her you're okay."

Zoë groaned louder and hid her face in her hands. "Please don't. Just let me stay here until I feel better."

Claudia looked toward Jeff. "What time is it?"

He checked his watch. "It's nine-thirty. Zoë, when did you take those drugs?"

All they could hear was a soft snore. Claudia sighed. "Perhaps if we wait an hour or so, she'll be recovered enough that we can take her home."

Jeff checked Zoë's pulse and her breathing, and said, "Here's a plan. Let's take her into the tent. It's all set up after all, and it looks like she got some pretty good equipment, so it's bound to be more comfortable than the ground outside. We'll check her carefully every half hour or so. And then we'll take her home around midnight, when it will be understandable that she's tired and needs to go straight to bed. But you should call your mom. She needs to hear that you found Zoë and that she's safe."

Claudia sighed again. "You're right. If my dad isn't there, I might even be able to ask her advice—"

Zoë wailed again, "No, don't tell Mom. She'll tell Dad."

"Hush!" Claudia moved off into the woods to make the phone call, while Jeff bent down to gather Zoë up and move her into the tent.

"Mom?" Claudia spoke softly into the phone. "Are you alone?"

"Darling! It's good to hear from you. Dad was just telling me about his day and asking about you."

"Well then, I'll just tell you the news. Zoë is safe. We're going to stay with her and bring her home later, maybe tonight around midnight. Leave the back door open and I'll get her into bed myself. Don't worry."

"That's so nice to hear, dear," her mother spoke gaily into the phone. "I'm glad you and Zoë are out together. Have a good time. We won't wait up for you."

"Thanks, Mom. Goodbye." Claudia put her phone away, and went thoughtfully back to where Jeff was now sitting patiently waiting for her to return.

"My mom is a good actress too." she said as she sat down beside him. "You should have heard her voice just now. I'm sure my dad was sitting right there next to her, and you would never know that there had ever been anything wrong. She's a master at this."

"Claudia, why are you all so afraid of your dad?"

"That's a very good question, Jeff. I have been trying to figure that out." She shook her head. "Well, you encountered it yourself, didn't you? When you had your meeting with him four years ago, why didn't you argue with him? Why didn't you just call me anyway?"

"Well, you know what your dad is like."

"Yeah, he's a scary guy, though he's never actually done anything to hurt me or any of us. Somehow he intimidates me into submitting. I don't know how. I keep trying to figure it out. And once I understand what's going on, I will be able to stop it. Because, I'll tell you, I'm sick of it." She sat up straighter and nodded her head. Tonight she had vanquished the dreaded druggies, and tomorrow she would stand up to her father. Maybe. She hoped.

"I'm glad, Claudia. I hate thinking that you are willing to go on this way forever."

Jeff put his arm around Claudia and she leaned back against him, finally relaxing for the first time since she had suddenly noticed that Zoë was gone the day before.

"Of course I'm not willing. But, it's complicated. I could put my foot down and leave tomorrow, but where does that leave Zoë? Nobody else is paying any attention to her, and you have to agree, she's teetering on the edge of serious trouble. I feel responsible."

"Yes, you're right about that. But your professor expects you, doesn't she?"

"She does. I guess I just have to solve all the world's problems before I go." Claudia gave a brief chuckle.

"Well, if anyone can do it, you can."

"You've got a lot more confidence in me than I do. Well, certainly more than my dad does."

"He doesn't compliment you very often, does he?"

"No, he doesn't. In fact, he had some pretty insulting things to say about my worth in the firm. I think he'd be pretty happy if he could just marry me off to the boss's son and get me out of his hair for good."

"The boss's son?"

Claudia averted her eyes. "Yes. My boss at my dad's firm is the son of one of the senior partners. You saw him at the country club sitting at our table. My father invited him. My parents think he's wonderful."

"So, what do you think? Do you agree with your folks? Is he wonderful?"

"No. I don't like him at all. He creeps me out. But, my mom thinks he would be a great catch. He's very good looking. He's rich. He's connected to power. And he'll undoubtedly make partner someday."

"Ah. He's ambitious. They like that in a man."

"Yes, they do. He's very smooth too. He knows just how to butter them up. My dad is mesmerized by his every word. And he seems to be interested in me. Though I don't know why."

"Well, that's an easy one to answer. You're beautiful and fun and interesting and smart. . ." and finally Jeff kissed her. His hungry mouth pressed down on hers, while he twined his fingers through her hair and pulled her head back to expose her soft neck. His kisses traveled down from her ear and onto the line of her collarbone. She gasped at the tickle of his lips on her body. Her hands tried to grasp his arms, but they merely fluttered helplessly and then fell to her sides. She shivered.

As she reached up to dig her fingers into his hair to pull his face to hers, all thought of Nathan Emerson disappeared from her mind.

CHAPTER 16

Claudia heard the buzz of her cell phone coming from under her desk even before it rang. It was a quiet afternoon, and she had already finished most of the typing that she had found in her inbox that morning. She grabbed her phone and whispered to Barbara, who was researching for a case at the corner table, that she was taking a break.

"Hello." she whispered as she walked quickly down the hall.

"Hi, Claudia," whispered Andi, matching Claudia's tone. "I was wondering about Zoë. Is she all right? Did she get in trouble with your dad? Was she with those guys that I saw the other day?"

Claudia filled her in on the happenings of the day before. "Then we snuck her into the house late, so my dad wouldn't see how wasted she was. That would have caused such a scene. My mom did her part too, convincing him we were all out together doing who knows what innocent thing. He didn't give us a second glance this morning —just got up, ate his breakfast, and left for work."

"He's not very curious about your lives, is he?" Andi wondered. "My dad would be asking for all the details just to make conversation."

"No," Claudia replied slowly. "That is surprising, isn't it? I'm used to him being rather intrusive, always wanting to dig into our lives so he can lecture us about how we're going about it the wrong way. Benjamin is the only one he doesn't criticize constantly."

"What do you suppose happened to make him change? Could he be learning to be more tolerant?"

"I doubt it." Claudia reflected. "Maybe something else is distracting him." She thought of the dark-haired beauty across the aisle at church.

"What could it be?"

"I don't know. But, I have to get back to work. Talk to you later." She disconnected the call, slid her phone into her handbag, and then went back to her typewriter.

An hour later, Claudia had finished typing a summary of a case that Nathan was working on with the senior Mr. Emerson. She had produced a copy that needed to be delivered to Mr. Emerson's secretary, whose office was down in the hallway with all the other partners in the firm.

She rarely saw her father during the day, and she didn't know what she would say if she did run into him. But she had business being there, and she was determined not to be embarrassed about conducting it. She walked down the long hallway past conference rooms and offices, her high-heeled shoes patting softly on the carpeted floor. There were subdued sounds of voices behind closed doors and the muffled sound of telephones ringing. Finally she rounded the corner into the vestibule of the suite of offices belonging to the senior partners of the firm. Her father's office was the first door on the right, she remembered, from a time long ago when she and her mother had come by to take her father out to lunch.

Claudia didn't intend to talk to her father. She just walked past his office on her way to deliver the document. But before she reached his door on her way back, it opened and she was surprised to see the same strikingly beautiful woman whom she noticed in church on Sunday. Claudia gasped and shrank back into the shadows. Peeking out of the darkness, she saw her father pull the woman back into the office with a hand on the back of her neck. Claudia just glimpsed the beginning of a passionate kiss before the door swung shut again. She turned trying to catch her breath and stumbled away. Finally she pulled herself together and ran as quickly as she could without drawing attention to herself back to her own desk in the other end of the building.

* * *

Home again, Claudia threw a load of laundry into the washer and headed up to Zoë's room. She had to see her sister and make sure she was okay after the ordeal of the last few days. She also needed to get her mind off of the sight she witnessed that afternoon in the doorway of her father's office. Was that really what she thought it was? She had to think very hard before she decided what to do with that information.

The room was cluttered as usual, with fast food wrappers and empty soda cans. There was a pile of school books on the desk, but none of the books were open. Zoë was lying on the bed with her head turned toward the wall.

"Zoë," Claudia ran across the room and sat down beside her. "What's the matter? Are you sick?"

"Don't you talk to me!" Zoë turned on her. "You've ruined my life!"

Claudia recoiled as though she had been slapped. "What? What happened? What did I do?"

Zoë's face crumpled. "I don't remember." She burst into tears.

Laughter threatened to bubble up, but Claudia held it down. "Why are you angry at me then?"

Now Zoë was weeping quietly, which made Claudia feel even more sorry for her. "Zoë, did something happen today at school?"

"None of my friends will talk to me. All I know is that a few days ago, I had a whole gang of friends, and now I've got NOTHING, and NO ONE. When I tried to sit by Ben and Tommy at the school rally, they yelled at me to get away, that they never wanted to see me or my sister again. They wouldn't explain, they just pushed me away. Everybody was laughing at me. I felt like a fool, and I didn't even understand why."

"Oh Zoë." Claudia sank down on the bed and reached out to Zoë. Zoë buried her face in Claudia's shoulder. "Those guys aren't good for you. They aren't real friends."

"But, they were all I had," Zoë wailed. "And now I have nothing."

Claudia sighed. "You have me."

All she could hear was a muffled sob. She patted Zoë on the back and gazed around the room. The afternoon sun was streaming through the window to the floor at her feet. She stretched out her feet and allowed the sun to warm them, while she stroked Zoë's hair. She tried to be a soothing influence but wondered if she might need it as much as Zoë did. Her father was having an affair with the secretary—or whoever that woman was. Her mother was beginning to break under the strain of pretending that her life was perfect. Her sister was in real danger of ruining her own life. Her studies were a mess, her social life was a mess, and she was doing drugs. How could Claudia fix all that? She felt completely out of her depth.

She cleared her throat. "Have you talked with Mom about these things?"

Zoë looked up in disbelief. "You think Mom would ever want to hear about my problems? Mom and Dad both just keep telling me to straighten up and quit screwing around. They have no idea what is going on in my life. And I don't think they want to know."

"Well then, let's you and me think about what you should do. We didn't do too badly before. We got Mom and Dad to get off your back, didn't we? Now we have to solve the problem of you needing more friends."

Zoë shook her head. "There is no solution for that. I'm not pretty like you. And I'm not smart and I don't fit in with any of the cliques at school."

"Poor sweetie," Claudia murmured soothingly. "You are such a unique and genuine person, I'm not surprised you don't feel comfortable with any of the cliques. They're all so superficial, and you don't play their games."

"I hate having to pretend."

"I know. That's what I most love about you."

"But how will I ever make friends if I can't put on at least some kind of act?"

"Zoë, you shouldn't have to pretend. You need to be yourself and find people who are fine with that."

"I thought I was being myself already."

"Is that look really you though? Seems to me you hide your true self when you paint your face with all that black. It puts people off. You know, you have a lot of natural beauty. If you just let it out, you'd be much more attractive. And that's not pretending."

Zoë raised her eyebrows and gave Claudia a doubtful smile. "Me, natural beauty?"

Claudia smiled broadly in return. "Yes! You've just been covering it up for so long you don't even know it's there." She hesitated a moment. "If you're interested, I can help you learn how to make the most of your looks."

"I don't know." Zoë spoke hesitantly. "It's all so weird and contrived if you have to work for it. I don't want to be a fake. I mean, look at Mom. We never even see her in her pajamas."

"I'm not expecting you to become like Mom, Zoë. You have to figure out what's best for you." Claudia said. "Once you do that, I bet you'll find that it's no more difficult than what you've been doing to prove that you don't care about your looks."

Zoë laughed at that. "Well…okay. What do I have to do?"

"First thing is you go take a shower. Wash your face really well, and then come out and put on some jeans and a t-shirt. I'm going to go make a phone call." She shooed Zoë out the door and headed down to the telephone.

Fifteen minutes later, Claudia called down to her mother not to wait dinner for them, and they headed out the door to the car.

An hour and a half later, Zoë was staring dumbstruck into the salon mirror. Claudia settled the bill and she and Zoë jumped back into the car.

"Now where are we going?"

"We're going to the mall."

Zoë didn't argue, but Claudia knew she was nervous. She didn't say anything else, just sat and looked out the car window.

By the time the stores were closing, the two sisters had bought makeup suggested by the lovely lady at the counter in the department store, and then a couple of new bras. They ended by getting several new outfits to show off the figure Claudia knew Zoë had, but had always hidden. Driving home, Claudia couldn't help but give her sister one last word of advice.

"Now, you're going to have to get up a little earlier in the morning, so you can put that makeup on. Do you think you can manage that?"

Zoë suddenly stopped smiling and looked terrified. "Claudia, I can't look like this in public!"

"Of course you can," Claudia assured her. "You just have to pretend you're the new girl at school, and you will be reintroducing yourself to everybody there. Are there any nice girls at all at your school? I don't mean popular or pretty. I mean nice."

"Hmmm. Well, yeah. There are some." Zoë admitted.

"Those are the girls you should try to talk to."

They pulled into the driveway, and got out of the car. Zoë hesitated.

"What's the matter now?" Claudia asked.

"Mom and Dad. They're going to think they won."

Claudia laughed at that. "It doesn't matter what they think. You're doing this for you. You know, Zoë, what you look like on the outside isn't who you are. It's just a costume. The costume tells people who you want to be taken for, so you can attract the same sort of people. When you dressed like a druggie, you got drug-dealing friends. Dressing like this might just get you a different sort of friend. I hope so anyway."

"I hope so too," Zoë said. "But do you think I'll ever have real friends? The way you and Andi are?"

"Sure you will. You're a sweet person. You just have to let it show."

CHAPTER 17

The next morning, Claudia got up earlier than usual so she could offer her help to Zoë if she needed it. She knew that a night of brooding could very easily make Zoë lose her resolve to get a fresh start. She was pleasantly surprised therefore when she peeked into the hall bathroom and found Zoë carefully applying the finishing touches of her new makeup on her cheeks. The results were striking, and Zoë looked like she even thought so too.

"Now listen," Claudia said. "This is who you are now. If anyone asks you where that old wilder you went, just shrug your shoulders and say that you were tired of all that black and decided it was time for a change."

Zoë smiled shakily at her reflection in the mirror. "Well, I'll try. But I don't think it's going to be that easy. People can be awfully mean."

Claudia hugged her, and headed back to her room to get ready for work.

While she was driving to work, Claudia's cell phone rang. It was Jeff.

"I wanted to catch you before work today and see how things are since Monday. Is Zoë doing okay?"

"Jeff, I'm sure glad to hear your voice. Yes, Zoë is quite recovered and we had some good girl time together yesterday." Taking a chance, Claudia finally brought up the subject she had been holding in until now. "Who I'm really worried about though is my dad."

"What's going on with him?"

"I think he's seeing another woman. And I don't know what to do about it."

"Your poor mother."

"Yes, but not just my mom. It's hurting the whole family. He's been so distant and unpleasant lately. Even going back to when I first got home. He's really critical of everyone, or he doesn't talk at all. He's gone a lot. My mom seems to be holding on by a thread, cooking his favorite meals, wandering around the house worrying how she's going to act when he gets home." Finally putting her fears into words, Claudia couldn't stop talking. "She's not the same person I remember. She seems so insecure, and that just isn't normal. I don't know if she suspects an affair, but she knows he's not interested in her anymore."

"Well, what makes you think it's an affair? Maybe he's just worried about his work."

"No, I saw him and this woman eyeing each other in church on Sunday. And then the other day, I was down near his office, and I saw that same woman in the doorway, and they were kissing."

"Well, there's not much you can say to explain that away, is there? I'd be surprised if your mom doesn't know about it."

"I'm not eager to bring up the subject with her. But I wonder if I shouldn't. If I were her, I sure wouldn't want to be kept in the dark."

"No, neither would I. But I wouldn't rush into anything. Once you let that cat out of the bag, there's no stuffing it back in."

Claudia smiled sadly as she pulled into the parking lot. "That's for sure." She nosed into a space far away in the back corner of the lot. "I'm at work now. I'm going to have to talk to you later."

"Okay. I'll call you this afternoon."

"Thanks. Uh, Jeff, don't talk to anyone about my dad."

"Of course not. You can trust me."

Claudia thought about the conversation as she walked into the building. She was surprised at how easily she had confided in Jeff the horrendous news about her father's possible affair. In the past, she never would have talked about anything that private with a friend, but somehow she felt like she needed some support, and Jeff was so solid and understanding.

As she walked into work, she couldn't help but think about the contrast between him and her go-getter boss. Nathan wore expensive suits. Jeff wore blue jeans and old t-shirts. Nathan had a commanding, high-stress air about him, Jeff was relaxed and confident. She felt good with Jeff, like she belonged with him. Nathan was exciting, but he made her uneasy. She felt like she could never be part of his world. Nor would she want to.

Claudia became aware of an undercurrent of excitement in the office. She looked questioningly at Barbara, who was bustling around gathering papers and heading out the door.

"Nathan is giving the closing arguments to the jury today for the Simonsen case. I'm going to go watch. Do you want to join me?"

Claudia looked at the pile of work on her desk. "I have so much to do, but it would be interesting. How long will it be?"

"An hour at the most. Nathan won't mind. In fact, he probably won't even see us. We'll be hiding in the back."

Making a snap decision, Claudia swung the strap of her purse back over her shoulder and followed Barbara back out of the building.

Claudia climbed into Barbara's car, excited. She had never been to court before, even though her father was a lawyer and regularly argued cases before the judge.

"Are you sure Nathan won't mind?"

"Of course, he'll be fine with it. He loves performing to an audience." Seeing Claudia's doubtful look, she added, "And it's very common for assistants and partners to go observe the cases they've had a hand in preparing. It gives us closure too. We deserve it."

When they slid into the last row of courtroom number three, she realized she had nothing to worry about. There were probably over sixty other spectators in the courtroom, most of them waiting for other cases, and the view she had of the back of Nathan's head was blocked by the large man sitting in front of her. Chances were that Nathan was never going to even notice that she and Barbara were there.

It was a relatively straightforward case. All Nathan had to do was explain to the judge how this insurance company had lied to the plaintiff in an effort to get out of an obligation to pay on a claim that was turning out to be an enormous sum of money. He had all the evidence he needed, and all the forms were in his briefcase to prove it. Claudia knew it because she had typed up the summary of the case and even the closing arguments that Nathan had prepared the week before. Sitting in the warm, crowded courtroom trying to pay attention was difficult for Claudia though, with so much else on her mind and so little sleep in the last few days.

Barbara dug her elbow into her side at one point, and handed her a stick of peppermint chewing gum.

"This might help you stay awake," she whispered.

Claudia took the gum gratefully and popped it in her mouth.

Nathan was just finishing his recitation of the bureaucratic shenanigans that the company had engaged in, and he was clearly searching the papers in his hands for his next point. "Umm, so, Your Honor, umm. . ." He rustled through his briefcase.

"Mr. Emerson, are you having trouble finding something?"

"No, I have it right here." He continued to search. Finally he pulled out a stapled sheaf of papers. Claudia recognized the report she had typed the week before.

The judge looked through the report and then turned to the lawyer for the insurance company. "You know this is the company's second attempt to avoid paying on this policy?"

"Yes, Your Honor."

"And that by the rules of this court, they are obligated to cover these bills?"

"Yes, Your Honor. But—"

"I'm making a summary judgment for the plaintiff." The gavel came down and it was over.

As they climbed into Barbara's car to head back to the office, Barbara asked Claudia, "So, what did you think of our illustrious leader?"

Claudia wasn't quite sure how to answer that. "I think I've seen too many law shows on television." She smiled apologetically.

Barbara snorted. "That's a kind way of saying that Nathan is not a very exciting speaker. But just wait and see. He's going to come back to the office all swagger and boast. So much of this job is just convincing others that we know what we're doing. If you can *act* big, then maybe you'll *be* big." She looked at the clock on the dashboard. "We have to get back to the office, but it's time for lunch. Do you want to stop and pick up sandwiches?"

Claudia nodded absently as she thought about what Barbara had just said.

* * *

They arrived back at work just after one o'clock. Walking toward the rear entrance to the building, Claudia caught a glimpse of her father and the beautiful mystery woman leaving through the same door. She murmured goodbye to Barbara and headed straight up to her office.

Early in the afternoon, just as Claudia had settled in to a large typing assignment, a messenger came around to tell them all that at two o'clock, everyone was to leave the building.

Claudia noted the time and kept typing.

Barbara stuck her head into the office. "You've heard about the fumigation?"

"What? Fumigation? What are they fumigating for?"

"Probably someone saw a cockroach in the bathroom or something. Just wanted to make sure you knew to leave by two."

Claudia grabbed her purse from the floor below her desk. "Auu-ugh." She shook it and then looked into the pockets, grimacing. "I hate cockroaches!"

She looked back up at Barbara. "Thanks. Yes, I'll get out in time."

Barbara snickered as she walked away down the hall.

Claudia arrived home well before her usual time. Walking into the house, she heard a clattering sound coming from the den. Following the noise, she discovered her mother taking down blinds for cleaning.

"Don't you ever relax?" Claudia said with a smile, helping her mother down from the stepladder.

Claudia's mother swiped at the hair that had fallen in her eyes. "Yes, but then I think of something else to do."

She looked at the clock. "What are you doing home so early?"

"Apparently, there are cockroaches in the building and we all had to get out so they could poison the little buggers."

"Well, then I'd better get this mess out of your father's room. He'll probably want to sit and work a while longer after he gets home."

Claudia helped gather the blinds that were lying on the floor and move them to the utility room. She vacuumed while her mother went for a bucket of cleaning solution, and then Claudia got herself a cup of tea and a brownie from the kitchen and settled herself in the living room with her book.

The afternoon passed peacefully. Claudia read, while the noises of her mother bustling around the house drifted into the room. Now and then, she would pass through and they would smile at each other.

Zoë came home around four thirty, dropped her coat on the floor of the front hall closet, and then headed up the stairs to her room. When Claudia followed her up and knocked on the door, all she got was an angry grunt. She gently tried the door, but it was locked, so she backed away and returned to her book.

At five, the phone rang. Claudia waited to see if it was for her, but she could hear her mother answering it in the next room.

"Yes?"

"Roger, I thought—"

"What time then do you—"

"Of course, honey, I—"

Claudia heard her mother hang up the phone slowly. A bad feeling came over her and when she looked up, her mother was standing in the doorway with a stricken look on her face.

"Mom, what is it?"

"Your father is at the office. He says he has to work all evening, and I shouldn't wait up."

Claudia gulped.

Her mother picked at a bit of fuzz on her sweater. "Was it the whole building that was going to be treated?"

"Yes, that's what I was told."

"But, maybe they weren't going to do the partners' hallway."

The page of Claudia's book was rustling. She looked down and forced her hands to be still. "Mom, Mr. Emerson walked out of the building with me."

"Well, you must have misunderstood." Her mother's voice became shrill.

"I know I didn't."

"How can you be so sure?"

"I saw Dad leave before we got the announcement. He was with that woman I saw in church."

Her mother's eyes widened with emotion. "What woman?"

"I don't know who she is. She was across the aisle and up a few rows. She had dark hair."

"That's just your father's secretary. I'm sure it was nothing." Speaking in a relieved voice, Claudia's mother straightened her shoulders and turned to go back into the kitchen.

"Mom?"

She stopped but didn't meet Claudia's eyes. "What?"

"I saw them kissing yesterday." She couldn't keep her voice from breaking. "I was down in his wing of the building. He didn't know I was there, and she was in his doorway, and he pulled her into his office and kissed her."

Her mother reminded Claudia of one of the deer that sometimes came to the edge of their property to nibble on the hosta. She knew she had to be very still so as not to scare her off.

"Mom? Are you all right?" Her mother was crying now.

She turned finally, looked straight into Claudia's eyes, and said, "I don't really know." She looked rather unsteady.

Claudia got up from her seat and rushed over to her mother. "Mom, come and sit down. I'll get you a cup of tea." She led her mother over to the easy chair, lowered her down, and then ran for the kitchen.

When she returned with a steaming hot cup of Earl Grey, her mother was quietly crying into her handkerchief. Claudia set the tea on the side table, sat down, and put an arm around her mother. As she sat there, patting her mother's back, she saw Zoë tiptoeing down the stairs with a terrified, questioning look on her face. Claudia shook her head. Zoë leaned against the bannister silently.

"I'm sorry, Mom," Claudia said.

"Why did you tell me?"

"I almost didn't. But finally I decided that if I were you I would want to know, especially if I had suspicions. You were beginning to wonder, weren't you?"

"I suppose I was. But you could have pretended. I just needed to hear a good excuse—be reassured."

"You can't tell me you wish I had left you in the dark! Don't you think knowing the truth is always best?"

Claudia's mother finally pulled away, wiped her eyes, and straightened out her apron. "Claudia, one thing you need to know about married life…you don't always want to know the whole truth, and sometimes a good believable story is really what you need to keep yourself together and keep your marriage intact."

Claudia sat there with her mouth open staring at her mother. "But…"

"Mom, that is just bullshit!" Zoë broke in.

"Zoë, shame on you!" Claudia gasped.

"I mean it! Mom, you can't just let him cheat on you! Everybody in town knows what's going on. It's time you did too."

"Everybody in town? Who do you mean?"

"Well, I bet everybody in church has noticed. Don't you think so, Claudia?"

"I'm sorry, Mom. He was being pretty obvious."

"Well, if I didn't see it, than how would anybody else notice?"

Zoë rolled her eyes and left the room.

"Mom, you had your eyes closed!" Claudia knew she had gone too far. "Maybe you're right."

Claudia's mother drained her tea and straightened herself visibly. "Now, thank you for worrying about me, dear, but it really is not necessary. I think I will go get dinner ready for the rest of us, since your father is working late, and we might as well eat soon."

"But…"

"Dear, why don't you go do some laundry or something?"

"I don't have any to do."

"Well, why don't you start one load for me. Or, rinse the bathroom sink. Just go do something!" Her voice sounded hysterical.

"Mom, what are you going to do?"

"What do you think I'm going to do? I'm going to go make some pork chops." She stalked into the kitchen and closed the door.

Claudia stood staring after her mother, then took her book up the stairs. As she passed Zoë's room, she knocked gently and heard Zoë whisper, "Come in."

"How on earth did that come up?" Zoë hissed.

"Don't repeat this to a single soul."

"Of course not."

Claudia explained about the cockroaches, and the early dismissal from work, and about her father's phone call long after Claudia saw him leave with the beautiful woman from church.

"I knew about her," Zoë said angrily. "That's why I hate to go to church with Mom and Dad. He's always making eyes at her."

Claudia gasped. "How long have you known about this?"

"Months." Zoë shrugged. "I haven't been to church since March, so I know it's been at least that long. Mom always keeps her eyes really tight shut, so she doesn't have to watch. I think she doesn't want to believe it's really happening."

"That's horrible!"

"But, Claudia, what would Mom do if she admitted the truth? Is she going to leave Dad?" she said derisively.

Claudia admitted she couldn't imagine the two of them ever splitting up. "But she should at least confront him…make him stop."

"Do you really think anyone could force Dad to do anything?"

"I don't know. But Mom shouldn't put up with it."

"But don't you see, Claudia, Mom isn't putting up with it. In her head, it's just not happening."

"But she's lying to herself!"

"Since when has that been important to this family? It's always been, 'what do other people think?' not, 'tell the truth.' You know it, Claudia. You've played along all your life. And you do it pretty well. That's why you can come home and fit right in, even after being gone for four years."

"And you aren't very good at it, so you are constantly getting in trouble."

"Exactly right." Zoë laughed bitterly.

"What about Benjamin?"

"Well, if you haven't noticed, he's the most successful of all, mainly because he's so smart and adds so much to the family's image. But I feel sorry for him. Because if he ever had a dream of his own, he would have no chance of following it."

Claudia thought of Benjamin's confession regarding his desire to go into general practice and nodded. "Zoë, you are very wise."

"Not so much, I don't think. Just because I can see what's happening, doesn't mean I have any power over it."

"It must be hard to be the youngest child, and be so aware of all the games that everybody else is playing." Claudia suddenly looked at Zoë, understanding. "And I bet this whole wild look of yours is your way of saying that you're just not going to join in their games with them."

Zoë shrugged uncomfortably. "Probably. Since I can't win trying to do things their way, I had to choose a different direction. But you were right about that. It's not really me either. I just couldn't figure out how to stop."

"How about now, though? How's your new look going over at school?"

Zoë grimaced. "Well, Claudia. I don't want to hurt your feelings since you were really just trying to help me, and I thought it was worth a try too. But…"

"But what?" Claudia had a sick feeling in the pit of her stomach.

"I will never have any friends. People were laughing at me—I could hear them. And since the other day in the woods, my old friends won't talk to me either."

"You can't switch back now, can you?"

"I don't know if I even want to. All that black *was* getting old. I just can't wait for the end of the school year. Just a little while longer, I keep telling myself."

"That's a sad thing to have to say. I really thought this would be good for you. And I've forced Mom against her will to see how bad her marriage is. I've made a real mess of things haven't I?"

"Well, I don't know that things would have lasted the way they were, anyway." Zoë glanced down at the books on her bed. "I think I'd better get back to my reading. I'm trying to pass my final exams."

"Do you want some help?"

"No, that's okay. I know what I have to do."

Claudia wandered into her own room to lie down. She didn't want to go downstairs and view the damage she had inflicted on her mother, but it was going to be dinnertime soon and she'd have to pull herself together to go pretend everything was fine again. Claudia was tired just thinking about it.

✳ ✳ ✳

Claudia awoke with a start. The clock showed eight thirty, and the light was getting dim. Her head felt groggy from the nap she had just taken, and her stomach was empty. Her mother hadn't awakened her for dinner. She couldn't remember a time when her mother did not serve a full meal to the entire family on the table at dinnertime.

She jumped out of bed and splashed her face with water to try to chase away the wooly feeling behind her eyes. The lights in the house were all darkened, and there wasn't a sound anywhere as she walked down the stairs and into the kitchen to look for something to ease her hunger.

She ate a pork chop in silence, feelings of dread and guilt hanging over her. She knew what she had seen. But was it really right for her to be the one to tell her mother about it? Who else, if not her? Someone had to do it. Claudia knew that she would want to know if it had been her husband fooling around with another woman. Besides, her father wasn't doing much to hide his actions. He had to know that Claudia might see what he was doing. Maybe he had a secret wish to have it all finally out in the open. Or maybe he just had no control over his urges and needed to be taught a lesson. Ha. Teach her father a lesson? Was it even possible?

In Claudia's eyes, her mother had always been strong and self-assured. Now she appeared fragile. Her father, on the other hand, was just as aggressive and unrelenting as he had ever been. In a showdown between her parents, she could not see anyone but her father coming out on top. What benefit was there in Claudia making it impossible for her mother to ignore all the clues to her husband's infidelity? Now that she had to confront the truth, the consequences could be horrible.

The offer from Professor Spencer tempted her more than ever at this point, though now she felt guilty at the thought of disappearing right after she had caused so much trouble for everybody else. That seemed rather childish and irresponsible to her. Didn't she owe it to her family to stay around and help clean up her mess?

Claudia was feeling uncomfortably passive and powerless. She had felt that way ever since she had returned home from college. It was fascinating to her, when she stepped back and observed the phenomenon, as though she really were an anthropologist instead of a player in the drama that was taking place. She had been out in the world on her own for four whole years. Her family had gone on as though she did not exist. Yet, now that she was home, she felt like a child again deep inside the family, and did not dare take a single step on her own for fear that she would get in trouble!

The complication that was Jeff Gordon was yet another puzzle. The physical attraction was back in all its force. Jeff seemed to have been struck with the same affliction, though it filled her with despair. She was leaving, and that would be that. Even if he loved her as much as she loved him, what could they do about it?

She wasn't sure what she wanted where Jeff was concerned. The thought of going back to school with a scholarship and a job in her favorite professor's lab was a dream come true for her. Studying her favorite subject further under a mentor like Donna Spencer meant that eventually she really would be able to work in the field of anthropology, to have her own place in the world, not just be a secretary for someone in a business she barely understood. On the other hand, being with Jeff again brought an ache to her heart that turned her into a quivering mess. She would love to stay in town long enough to see where that relationship could go.

CHAPTER 18

Jeff carried his toolbox and a 500-foot roll of Romex cable into the half-built mansion and headed down to the circuit box he was building in the basement. Through the open wall studs, he saw Stewart Mills in the distance talking with the project boss. Jeff didn't have the heart to banter with Stewart today. He ducked his head and hurried to his work. Luckily he had done this business for so long he could probably wire up a new house in his sleep. He had a lot on his mind and wanted the time to sort it out.

His mind was in a turmoil. When he first glimpsed Claudia through the window of Josie's Grill and realized that she was back, it had completely unsettled him. Life had been rather smooth up until now. He had his own house and a pretty comfortable circle of friends, and he was good at his craft. People admired him. The only thing missing was love, but he was young and figured he was in no hurry. It wasn't until Claudia returned and he started seeing her again that he began to wonder if it was time to do something about that.

Things between the two of them seemed to be going really well. They'd seen each other several times in the past couple of weeks and had some intensely intimate moments. It felt good. Really good. But it also brought him emotional distress that he simply wasn't used to. He needed to think.

What did he see in Claudia? And why hadn't he seen it in anyone else in the past four years? There was no shortage of women in this town, and he did get out now and then. He wasn't a monk after all.

As he drilled holes in the studs to draw wires through to the electrical boxes, he added up her good qualities. Her looks, of course. She had such thick bouncy hair, in a rich auburn color that glinted gold in the sunlight. She had a way of pushing it back that made him want to dig his fingers through it and bury his face in it. Her eyes were soft brown with a hint of green around the edges. When Claudia was concentrating on something, they squinted at the corners and her forehead furrowed so that he wanted to feather kisses all over her face. She did it unconsciously. He was sure she wasn't intentionally trying to drive him crazy. That would just be shallow.

And there was one thing Claudia was not, and that was shallow. Even in high school, when everyone's main purpose for being was to become popular and get people to "like" them, Claudia had seemed like a truly genuine person. Her reactions to events around her were always totally natural—unstaged. He always could tell what she thought just by watching her face. She was kind to everyone, and yet, she had shown him from the beginning that she thought he was special—special in a way that he didn't even understand.

Jeff felt ordinary. He was just a home-town boy who went to work the day after his high school graduation. She was from a wealthy family with a powerful father. And she was a college girl too. How could she see anything in him? She had seen much more of the world than he had. Her interests ranged in a direction he couldn't even talk about. He had thought, maybe naively, that now that she was home, they might be able to pick up where they left off, or at least make a new start and fall in love again.

But then, the other day she had let drop the news that she was going back to college. Graduate school would take up several more years and he didn't think that he could stand watching her go away like that again. What was even worse was seeing her in the country club with that sophisticated guy in the two-thousand-dollar suit. When he glimpsed the two of them sitting together at the table with Mr. and Mrs. Gilmore, Jeff had just stood there dazed. There he was in his coveralls, with spider webs smeared into his hair (which he found when he got home to take his second shower of the day), carrying a big box of tools. He was so obviously unsuited to be with a girl like Claudia. How could he even hope to be accepted into a family like that?

Yet she liked him. He could tell that she wasn't pretending. He didn't quite understand why, but he knew he could believe it. She was always ready and willing whenever he called, and the other day when she was in trouble, he was the one she called. She trusted him with her problems and respected his opinions. It's a good feeling when someone you love looks up to you. Even though she was smart and curious about the world, she still enjoyed the simple things, like sitting together under a tree in the woods in the dark listening to the owls hoot. He just didn't think the pleasant little activities he had to offer were going to be enough to hold her here. It might be that, as cruel as her father was to point it out, Jeff wasn't the right man for Claudia, and that he should step aside so she could pursue her higher intellectual and societal goals.

The more Jeff thought along these lines, the more agitated he became, until he stripped the nut on a wire clamp. He had to dig out the broken clamp and replace it, which took an extra ten minutes. That was when he realized that he could not accept Claudia leaving him again. He had to fight for her loyalty, even if it meant that he could lose. He would never forgive himself if he didn't even try.

* * *

After their companionable visit to the courthouse, Claudia and Barbara's relationship became more relaxed. They went to coffee together in the morning. They smiled at each other in passing. The tension Claudia had felt that first day was gone, and it seemed like they had been working together for much longer than the few weeks it had actually been.

One afternoon, Barbara came to the office with an amused expression on her face. She glanced up and down the hallway before closing the door, and sitting down to whisper in a conspiratorial fashion, "Have you heard?"

Claudia looked at her questioningly.

"Nathan won his case."

"Well, we knew that already, right?"

"Of course. But, you know, it wasn't a difficult case, and we were all sure that it would go his way. But now he's strutting around like a peacock, like he's another Perry Mason, charming juries and crushing his opposition with insightful revelations. Anyway, let him think he's hot stuff. It does keep the air pleasant around here." She winked and walked out.

Claudia had a smile on her face as she went back to her typing. It was still there when Nathan strode triumphantly by her office.

"I hear that I should congratulate you," she said looking up.

Nathan halted, surprised, then recovered. "Yes, I won! I'm thinking of taking the whole group out to D'Angelo's tonight for drinks to celebrate. I hope you'll be coming."

Claudia thought for a moment. She didn't really want to go anywhere with Nathan, but if everybody else was there too, it might be fun. She hadn't had many opportunities to talk to the other people in the office. "I believe so. Yes, I can be there."

Nathan pointed a finger at Claudia. "I'll see *you* then, at nine o'clock." He sauntered away, stopping every now and then in the hallway to chat with others. Claudia watched through the window before she turned back to her work. Since Nathan's case was now over, there was only a little bit left to do to put that file away, forms to fill out, bills to be sent. She still had to work on ongoing cases for Barbara. Nathan had a few others coming up too, though he hadn't been working on them with much enthusiasm yet, since all his attention was taken up by the Simonsen case.

Before she began working in the law office, Claudia knew very little of what went on there. Her only clue came from what she knew of her father, which wasn't much. Her mother had always led her to believe that her father was brilliant and important. Her father did not discourage that impression. She still didn't know how he spent his days at work, but she was getting to know Nathan, and from typing up all his correspondence she realized that there was a lot to legal work that was very dry and routine. Those were the aspects of the job that she unfortunately found herself most involved with. Boilerplate wills, and patent claims, custody disputes, and trust documents. Many of these documents had templates already existing, and she merely had to download them and insert unique and identifying information to tailor them to the specific case at hand.

Even when a case went to court, like this one which made everybody so excited and Nathan so proud, it was mostly a matter of organizing the material and then presenting it in a rational order. The image that television law shows presented was so much more impressive than was actually the case. It wasn't distressing to Claudia. In fact, that made her role in the process easier to take. Knowing that carrying out almost any assignment was straightforward made it all much less frightening.

When she had a neat pile of completed work on the corner of her desk, she leaned back to stretch her tired muscles. A satisfying crack immediately gave her relief, and she got up to walk around the office to file. In the relative quiet of the empty room, a tinkling melody emanated from her cellphone.

"Hi Andi." She saw by the clock that it was break time, so she held the phone with her shoulder while she poured herself a cup of coffee and swiveled her chair around so she could put her feet up on the edge of the trash can.

"Jeff was in this afternoon picking up supplies. What happened between the two of you? He looked like a thundercloud. He didn't even say hi to me until I had been standing in front of him for a full minute."

Claudia swallowed a sip of her coffee, and tried to search her memory. "I don't know. The last time I saw him, he was dropping me and Zoë off at my house late Monday night. And then I talked to him this morning on the way to work. I thought things were going well."

"So, you haven't had a fight or anything lately?"

"I forgot. But that was before. Monday we got along fine."

"What was before? Anything you want to share with me?"

"Well." Claudia quickly looked at the door, to make sure no one was about to surprise her. "My family went to the country club for brunch on Sunday, and it turned out that he was there doing a job of some sort. But I didn't notice him until we were sitting down eating. My father had invited my boss, believe it or not, to come sit with us. And then when I saw Jeff across the room, he was pretty angry. We had words."

"Your boss? Why would that make Jeff mad?"

Claudia knew no one was listening, but she leaned down to whisper anyway. "He's pretty good-looking. Jeff happened to see Nathan talking with his hand on my arm. I think he's being totally unreasonable, but you know how men can be."

"Ah. Well, that explains it."

"But, I don't even like my boss. He's too much like my dad. And I told Jeff that. Then, the next day, things were fine. He helped me find Zoë, and we got in some good cuddling and kissing while we were waiting outside Zoë's tent for her to sleep off her high."

"Maybe he's been brooding since then, and can't get it off of his mind. Maybe he is madly in love with you, and is getting nervous about his competition."

Claudia tapped the desk with a pencil. "Or maybe he just had a fight with the supervisor on the job. It doesn't always have to be about love."

"But, it usually is." Andi chuckled softly.

"But really, we've had fun together. Even when I told him about grad school, he was angry, but he didn't confess any great undying love."

"Wait a minute!" Andi said in shock. "What about grad school? You haven't told me anything about that."

"It's a long story."

"Meet me at the Chocolate Kitchen. We can ruin our appetites for dinner together and you can tell me everything."

✳✳✳

Claudia sprinkled more cinnamon on her hot chocolate, and took another bite of her croissant. Andi was munching through a couple of very large, very gooey double chocolate chip cookies.

"I see how you can't decide what to do, Claudia." She swallowed one bite and took another one, crumbs spraying the table. "You have the two main men in your life, three really, if you count your boss, all acting like you're going to be around forever, and none of them considering your feelings at all."

"Well, I did come back. They might feel justified in thinking that I am back for good."

"But, I can't understand your father. You'd think that he'd be proud of you for getting such a compliment from your professor, and for being offered a scholarship too! That's really wonderful."

"I can't understand him either." Claudia's eyes misted over. "It just doesn't make any sense. Here I could be studying and publishing, and he'd rather I stay in a menial job and flirt with the senior partner's son."

"He'd probably love it if you married someone rich and successful just like him so he can show you off to all his high class friends."

"Yes." Claudia frowned. "But I don't want to marry someone just like him."

"Your mother seems like she's pretty satisfied with her position in society. Maybe it wouldn't be so bad." Andi popped the last bite of cookie in her mouth and finished her hot chocolate with one last gulp.

"She hasn't been so happy lately. It seems my dad is having an affair."

"Oh my god, how awful. I'm sorry. Do you think she knows?"

"Well, she does now." Claudia winced. "I told her."

"Well." Andi leaned back and gazed steadily at Claudia. "So, that's settled then. What made you decide to do that?"

"It wasn't really a decision." Claudia related the story about the fumigation and her father's excuse for not coming home.

"Claudia, it's his own fault. You have nothing to feel guilty about."

"What makes you think I'm feeling guilty?"

"Look at you. You have it written all over your face. Besides, I know you. You're tearing yourself up inside wondering if you did the right thing."

"You're right. Because when Mom got that call, she knew. And she quizzed me, and I could have lied right there, which was exactly what I think she wished I would do. She didn't want to have to face it. And I'm not sure what she's going to do with that knowledge. I've never seen her confront my father. He's a hard man to talk to."

"I see why you're afraid of him, Claudia. He's a bully. And you've always been under his power. But you don't have to stay there. You can leave now. Go away, get back to your studies, be an adult again. Right? That's what you want to do, isn't it?"

"Yes, more than anything."

"Then that's settled."

"But, I want to stay too, and see whether Jeff loves me, and whether we can make a go of it."

"But Claudia, you can't get married and live here, and go to grad school too."

"That's the problem."

"And Jeff is settled. He gets a lot of good work, and everybody knows him, and he has his own house and his own business. He's a great success."

"Yes. And he's never lived anywhere else. I can't imagine him deciding to pull up his roots now, just to follow me around."

"So, if you can't have both, you have to decide. I think that you'll never be satisfied if you don't go for it."

"I think you're right," Claudia said sadly. "But I think I love him."

"I know you do. But you need this. You can't live on love alone. You're an intellectual, Claudia. I've always known that about you. I can't imagine you being happy even doing what I do. But especially having to watch others go do the fun stuff while you sit and type for them. You're not happy."

"That's for sure."

Claudia knew how true Andi's words were. It was time to steel her heart and just go. Donna Spencer was expecting her soon, and she had known all along that she did not want to pass up this chance at getting away from her father's expectations of her, and going out to pursue her dream. Besides, she didn't seem to be doing a whole lot of good here. She might as well leave and let the others sort it all out themselves.

As for Jeff, she did love him, but if she was going to have to give everything up to be with him, she knew she would not last long. Better to make a clean break of things.

She sighed. "Well, thanks for helping me think things through, Andi. I know what I have to do now."

* * *

Though Claudia dreaded sitting down to dinner, she was surprised to find her mother setting the table for five. A pleasant scent was coming from the kitchen.

"Go clean up, dear, we're going to eat soon," her mother told her.

"I'm on my way." She furrowed her brow in confusion as she climbed the stairs to her room. *Are we back to pretending everything is just fine and dandy?* She washed her hands and scrubbed her face and changed out of her work clothes.

"I'm going out again tonight," she announced as she sat down at her place.

Her father unfolded his napkin onto his lap and asked, with a quietly threatening look on his face, "It's the middle of the week, Claudia. You have to work in the morning."

"Yes, this is for work, actually. Nathan invited us all out for drinks tonight to celebrate winning his case."

"Then that's different. Of course, you should go."

Of course I should go if it's Nathan I'm going to see! Claudia almost wished she had plans with Jeff, just so she could practice being strong in the face of her father's disapproval. She took a breath and turned toward Benjamin, who was quietly dishing up his broccoli, "Benjamin, how are things going with you? Weren't you just getting started on applications for internships?"

Benjamin seemed to recognize what she was trying to do, and obligingly launched into a long recitation of all the schools and programs he was considering or was in the process of or had already sent applications to. Thus, Claudia was able to eat peacefully throughout the meat and salad courses. Only when her mother rose to clear the plates and bring in dessert, did her father suddenly look up and say, "What?"

Benjamin repeated what he had just said. "I'm looking into the family practice program at the University of Cincinnati."

"Family practice?" Claudia's father's voice was deceptively calm.

"Yes."

"Why?"

"I'm interested in it."

Claudia and Zoë met each other's eyes, and then quickly looked down at their plates. An explosion was about to happen, and Claudia could not believe that her big brother, the golden boy, the one who was always good and never challenged their father's authority, was sticking his neck out and drawing all the fire toward himself.

Benjamin's gaze was steady and sure, her father's was piercing. The silence was deafening.

"Well, of course, you'll go to Princeton, when you get accepted there."

"Actually, Dad," Benjamin paused casually to take a bite of apple pie. "My preference is the program in Cincinnati."

Claudia felt like cheering, but she kept her face turned down. She poked her pie with her fork. She was so nervous that she could not bring herself to take a bite. Her father's face darkened like a thundercloud.

"So, you've decided to waste your education on the most mundane, the most pedestrian of specialties, when you could have your pick of the most prestigious programs in the country."

Benjamin looked up with determination, an expression Claudia did not recognize on him. He was finally going to speak his mind. She wanted to cheer.

"Prestige is not my main goal, Dad," he replied firmly. "I am thinking about my career."

"If you care about your career, Benjamin, you should go to the best school you can find."

"This is a very good program for family practice. And that's what I've decided to specialize in."

"Well, we'll talk about that."

"There's nothing to talk about Dad. It's my choice to make."

"That's where you're wrong. I'm your father, and my opinion should prevail."

"I do recognize that you're my father, but this is my life. And therefore, I'm the one who has to make this decision."

Zoë was watching this interchange with her mouth hanging open. Claudia, thrilled but also apprehensive, couldn't take her eyes off of her brother.

Her mother sat statue-like, holding the pie server in mid-air, but suddenly she came to life again. "That is very true, Benjamin." She served him another piece of pie, even though he was only halfway through with the one on his plate. "It is your life. I'm glad to see you taking charge of it."

Four sets of eyes turned to stare at her. Benjamin said, "Thank you, mother. I had hoped you'd feel that way."

Claudia's father sputtered. She wondered if she should bring up the subject of graduate school again. She figured that he was already as perturbed as he could be, so one more shock wouldn't make much difference.

"Ahem," she cleared her throat.

"This does not concern you!" Her father snapped in her direction.

"No, I know." Her voice was shaking, but she continued. "But I thought I'd mention that I've decided to take the offer to go to graduate school in the fall. In fact, my professor wants me there as soon as I can get there."

"I forbid you to go! You are going to stay at the firm and continue working for Nathan Emerson."

"Dad," Claudia protested, "I've been offered an assistantship. You don't have to pay for my school any more. I thought you'd be glad that I will not be wasting my education. My professor thinks I'm good! Why can't you be proud of me?"

"Listen! I supported you while you twiddled your thumbs for four years getting a useless degree in that glorified day camp they call a college out east. Now you want me to cheer you on while you go waste another four years working for crumbs and a few little perks. And for what? What comes next? You'll be coming home looking for a job, but you'll be four years older, that much less marketable, both in employment, but also in marriage, which means you'll be back here contributing nothing, but expecting me to take care of you. I got you a job, now you're going to stay and make yourself valuable to the firm. That's the way to get ahead in this world. You have to stick around long enough for people to begin to depend on you. Be reliable. Show you're worth something."

Claudia had held her head high throughout her father's tirade, and kept her eyes on his. When he finished, red-faced and out of breath, she simply replied, "I'm very sorry you see things that way. I had hoped that I could go with your blessing."

"You're not listening to me. You may not go!"

Claudia folded her napkin and placed it on the table. She stood up to leave.

"This conversation isn't over!"

"It is for me." Claudia walked out.

Claudia left the room. She was shaking, but she wasn't going to give her father the satisfaction of seeing her break down. Up in her room, she closed and locked the door. Her mind was racing. Now, more than ever, she was determined to leave.

But she needed a plan. The semester wouldn't begin until late August, and it was still early June. That would give her time to earn a little money to help her move out and find a new place to live. The first thing to do would be to fill out that paperwork and get it in the mail. Claudia sat down at her desk and started writing.

CHAPTER 19

When Claudia walked into D'Angelo's, she looked around, expecting to see her coworkers grouped together around a table. Instead, the bar was relatively quiet, with only a few people scattered around. As she stood there, trying to get her bearings, the hostess approached and asked, "Are you Claudia?"

"Yes, I am."

"Please follow me."

The woman led Claudia toward a booth in the far corner of the restaurant. On the table was a dish of shrimp cocktail. To her surprise, Nathan Emerson was the only person seated there, and he was looking up at her expectantly. When she reached the table, he leaped out of his seat to greet her.

"I'm glad you came."

"Thank you. I've been looking forward to it." Claudia spoke politely, but she was confused. "Where are the others?"

"Please, have a seat." Nathan indicated the bench across from his.

Once they were both seated and Claudia had ordered a glass of wine, Claudia was disconcerted to find Nathan's whole attention on her.

"I've wanted to get you away from work. It seems like we could have much to say to each other without the distractions of the day."

"Uh huh," Claudia said apprehensively. "I…I thought you had invited the whole group."

"Don't worry. We can pull some other tables up when they come."

Claudia took a sip of her wine and leaned back against her seat. "So, you must be feeling good about your case. That was quite a success."

Nathan looked gratified. "Yes, it feels good." Then he struck a blasé pose. "Of course, I expected to do well. I had some good arguments going in. And I could see the judge was eating up every point I made. The other guy just didn't have the moves."

Claudia hid her amusement behind her wine glass. Barbara's prediction was right on. Nathan's shakiness in court had been quite apparent, but he probably didn't want to remember that.

"I would have been nervous," she said innocently.

"Of course you would." He might as well have patted her on the head, for the attitude he was taking! "But remember, I've been doing this for several years now, and I was raised by one of the leading lawyers in the city. I've been in and out of courtrooms since I was a kid."

"Really?" Claudia thought of her own father, who had never mixed his family life with his law practice. Her father had never taken his children to court. "Are you serious? When you were a child, your father let you come watch his cases?"

"Sure. He knew we were curious, and seeing the real thing was a lot more accurate and educational than if we watched *Law and Order* every night on television."

"Well that makes a lot of sense." She said it matter-of-factly, but she felt a bit wistful, as she thought about what it might have been like if her father had ever shared that part of his life with his family.

"You're a lawyer's daughter. Didn't you ever go to the courthouse to watch?"

"No, never."

Nathan chuckled patronizingly. "I guess I was just more serious than most. My father didn't have a choice. I've always known I was meant to be a lawyer. I used to come home from school and argue cases with my dad at the dinner table. Even back then, he used to say that I'd be a formidable opponent someday. And now I'm proving him right."

She didn't know if she should apologize for not being interested in practicing law, or if maybe she shouldn't have admitted never going to the courthouse in the first place. Somehow, blaming it all on her father didn't seem appropriate either, though it did seem like he could have taken her if it was the right thing to do. So, she resorted to the time-honored way of getting out of a tough conversation. She changed the subject.

"So Nathan, where is everybody else? I thought you had invited the whole office out tonight."

"Actually," Keeping his eyes on her, Nathan took a shrimp from the plate and popped it into his mouth. "I may have given you the wrong impression there. I wanted to celebrate with you alone. Are you disappointed?"

Claudia felt a flash of anger, but steadied her nerves and replied with a nonchalant shrug. "I'm just surprised. I never thought we had anything but a professional relationship."

"Of course. And I admire you for keeping your work separate from your private life," Nathan said with a slightly mocking tone. "But, outside of work, you must enjoy letting your hair down and having some fun once in a while."

Claudia nodded, "Yes, fun is good. Though, it depends on what kind of fun you have in mind."

Nathan leaned forward and took her hand in his. "Is it that hard to tell? Don't tell me you are that naïve."

She narrowed her eyes. "I wouldn't say naïve, though I do like to assume the best of people until I am forced to admit otherwise." She pulled her hand away and put it in her lap. "Please don't make me think badly of you."

"Never! My goal tonight in fact is to do the very opposite!"

Claudia could feel her face flushing with irritation. This evening was turning out to be very different from what she expected. "Nathan …"

"Just relax. Let's just enjoy the evening."

Claudia looked at her watch. "Well, it's been lovely, but it's getting late. I really didn't expect to be out long. I'm pretty tired."

Nathan frowned. "You just got here."

"Nathan, if you had wanted to take me out on a date, you should have asked. Then I would have had a choice."

"What are you afraid of?"

"I'm not afraid, Nathan. I just am really not interested in the same thing you seem to be."

"What do you think I'm interested in?" he leered.

Claudia didn't answer his question. "I have to be at work tomorrow morning, and I'd like to go home and get some sleep."

Nathan was sputtering. Claudia gathered up her purse, and slid out of her side of the booth. She paused long enough to lay a ten-dollar bill down on the table and then she walked away as fast as she could. As she reached the front door of the restaurant, she glanced back and realized that Nathan had also thrown some money on the table and was now following close on her heels. Before she had a chance to say anything, he had grasped her arm and pushed her the rest of the way outside.

He was strong. There was nothing to grab onto once they were past the door. Rather than fall on her face, she allowed herself to be propelled down the steps and into the parking lot. The darkness outside was only broken by streetlights scattered around the cars. She began to feel panicky about being outside in the dark with someone she found she didn't know.

"Wait a minute!" She dug in her heels and glared at him. "Let go of me!" She said loudly.

"Can I help you, honey?" Two men who had been standing in the shadows, talking, stepped forward.

Nathan let go of Claudia's arm and stepped back away from her. "I was just talking to her," he mumbled angrily.

"Thank you," Claudia smiled gratefully at the beefy middle-aged man who had spoken to her. "If you would stay here with me a while, I was about to say good bye to Mr. Emerson and watch him drive away."

Both men stepped forward and crossing their arms in front of their chests. They stared menacingly at Nathan. Nathan stomped to his car, fumbled with his key, climbed in, and drove away.

Claudia stood quietly watching as his taillights receded into the distance. She thanked her self-appointed protectors again. While they watched, she got in her own car, and then took off in the opposite direction from Nathan's. Though she had managed to stay calm and steady at the restaurant, she felt shaky now. She did not really believe that Nathan would have harmed her. But the pounding of her heart, and the throbbing in her arm where he had grabbed her, reminded her of the fear that had gripped her there in the parking lot. She had been lucky someone had been nearby to help her, but she shouldn't need a hero. It just wasn't right that she was just beginning to learn how to assert herself with her father, and now was being forced to do the same with her pushy boss.

She should never have come back to Carlsburg. She could have looked for a job right there at the university, or at least nearby. She had come home because her father had made an arbitrary decision that she should give up on her education and come home to do what exactly? Get a job? Get a husband? She knew for sure that she had no interest in Nathan, especially now that he'd shown such an ugly side to her. Even if she thought he was handsome, which he was, and smart, which he must be, since he made it through law school, she knew she would not stand for that kind of sneaky, manipulative, arrogant man.

Jeff was so sweet in comparison. But, even Jeff didn't seem to believe that she would ever be strong enough to choose her own way in life. He pushed her to confront her father about going to grad school instead of trusting her to do things in her own time. She hated that he saw her as being weak. Come to think of it, their early relationship consisted of Jeff making all the decisions and Claudia following his lead. She didn't see that things had changed much in the intervening years either. Sure, they had fun, but it was always fun that he planned. Couldn't they ever do something she had thought of herself? Just because she couldn't actually think of anything herself, well, that wasn't her fault, was it? Maybe having all these men around making all the decisions for her was keeping her from having her own opinions. Maybe she'd have an opinion if she ever got away from the clamor of those who believed they knew better than she did what she should be doing with her life!

By the time Claudia got home, she had worked herself up into such a state of vexation that she would have snapped at anyone. Unfortunately, Jeff was the one who drove up to the curb not five minutes after she had.

Claudia was just beginning the job of packing her suitcases. Though she was tempted to just stuff everything in and run out the door, she folded her clothes carefully, when the doorbell rang. She heard it, but she decided to ignore it for now. When Zoë called her name from the front hallway, she almost swore out loud, she was so agitated. But she took a deep breath and headed down the stairs.

"Hello, Jeff." Her voice was colder than she had intended.

"Claudia." Jeff sounded uncharacteristically insecure.

"Claudia," he began again, then he looked at Mrs. Gilmore, who was standing to the side watching. "Could we go for a little walk? I'd like to talk to you."

Her mother pursed her lips together and shook her head as she walked away.

"That will be fine Jeff." She led him outside and around to the back yard.

They walked quietly without speaking, and when they reached the trees in the back of the lot, Claudia turned toward Jeff. She crossed her arms over her chest.

Jeff hesitated then reached into his pocket, and took out a small jeweler's box. He took one step back and lowered himself down to one knee. Gazing at the box in his hands, he began, "Claudia, since you've been back, I have realized that you're the one I've been waiting for. Living my life without you just will never be right. We belong together. Will you marry me?"

Claudia tried not to look at the ring. All she could think was, *Damn. Why can't I be trusted to pick my own ring?* Looking down at Jeff's earnest eyes, she felt love stirring in her heart. But still, she reminded herself that just ten minutes before, she was feeling truly sick of men telling her what she should do with her life, and what was best for her. As much as she wanted to cry out that, yes, they were right for each other, she still felt a strong sense of exasperation that he felt he needed to tell her that.

She reached out her hand to touch the ring lightly, then she closed the box and pressed it back into Jeff's palm. The pain in Jeff's face then was almost unbearable for her, but she steeled herself and said, "I'm sorry, Jeff. But I've decided you were right. I need to take charge and stop letting other people make all my decisions."

"But...but, that's not what I meant!"

"No, I know you didn't. You meant for me to stop letting my dad run my life. But trading him in for you won't make me strong either. I have to leave. You may not understand my choice. It seems selfish of me, I know. But I can't just keep doing what I'm expected to do. I have to direct my own life. Even if it makes me uncomfortable and I end up not fitting in with the people I've always considered my friends."

"But," Jeff said bitterly, "you'll have new friends to fit in with—if that's the life you want."

"I know that," Claudia said sadly. "But it doesn't make it any easier to remind myself of that."

Jeff tried one more time. "Claudia, you don't need to go. Don't you think we fit together well?"

"I do! But Jeff, this is who I need to be. It's who I am meant to be! And you...you're here. How can we get married if I'm going to be halfway across the country?"

Jeff didn't answer. His sad eyes told her that he thought it was just as hopeless as she thought it was.

"So that's that."

She nodded wordlessly.

With that, he turned on his heel and strode away, stuffing the ring back in his pocket.

Claudia watched him go, tears in her eyes. She hated having to reject his offer of marriage. She knew she'd love to be married to Jeff. He was so sweet to her, and she felt so comfortable with him. She could really picture herself spending the rest of her life with him, but she couldn't see staying here in Carlsburg forever. Maybe once she had finished her education so that she could get the kind of job where she would be contributing something important, and not just working to earn money. The tears flowed down her cheeks unchecked while she walked slowly back to the house.

CHAPTER 20

Friday morning was sunny and clear. As Claudia drove in to work, she realized with relief that this would be her last day. She hadn't been there long, so she knew she wouldn't miss anyone. She doubted that they would miss her. She had done a good job, learning the law business. She was a neat and meticulous worker, just as she was in all her classes at the university. In her work as a secretary, her typing was fast and flawless, and her presence in the office was quiet and unobtrusive.

When she arrived, she took the letter of resignation she'd written late the night before, photocopied it, and laid a copy on each of the Mr. Emersons' desks. Then she quickly typed up the work that was in her inbox and went to find a couple of empty boxes so she could pack up the few belongings that had collected in her drawers. Claudia was just finishing taping up the two boxes when she looked up to see Barbara leaning against her desk, anger on her face.

"What did he do to you?" Barbara said, indicating the boxes on the floor.

"I'm going to graduate school."

"Congratulations. But that's not why you're packing up today." Obviously Barbara wasn't going to accept anything but the truth.

Claudia sat back down in her chair. She sighed. "You're right."

Barbara waited.

Claudia sighed again. "Barbara. Yesterday. Did Nathan say anything to you about going out to celebrate his win in court?"

Barbara narrowed her eyes. "No. What did he tell you?"

"I really thought we were all invited. But when I got there…"

"Where?"

"D'Angelo's."

"So, when you got there…" Barbara prodded.

"He was there alone, at a table for two, waiting for me."

"He's scum, you know."

"Yes, I know that now. So, I stayed long enough to be polite, and then I got up to leave. He followed me outside and got aggressive. Thanks to a couple of guys in the parking lot, nothing else happened though, and he drove away."

Barbara's face was thunderous. "You have to tell your father at least."

Claudia smiled wryly. "I'm afraid that won't do any good. My father thinks Nathan can do no wrong. And what's more, my father is not very happy with me right now."

"But he surely wouldn't want you to be assaulted!"

"I doubt if he would see it as an assault. He would probably just insist that I misinterpreted things. Besides . . ."

Barbara quickly shut the door to the office, and came back to Claudia's desk, this time, sitting down to face Claudia directly. "Tell me."

"Can I trust you?"

"Of course. I am very good at keeping my mouth shut."

"I think my father is having an affair with someone I've seen in his office."

"You're right."

Claudia started. "What?"

"I'm just saying, yes, he is having an affair."

"You knew?"

"It's hard to hide an office romance for long."

"Who is that woman?"

"Cherise Baldwin. She's your father's administrative assistant."

"She's married, isn't she?"

"Yes. Her husband's a manager at the BMW dealership on Route 43, just on the east end of town. A nice enough guy, but apparently he works very long hours, so she's available a lot of the time. We don't see him much, even at the office Christmas party where all the spouses are invited."

"And everybody knows about her and my dad?"

"Except for the ones with their heads in holes in the ground. Some people manage to stay completely innocent of what's going on around them. But there aren't many people like that around here."

Claudia was stunned. Here was information that her mother had only just discovered, or was made to face, that apparently numerous other people had been aware of all along. As she pondered this, she felt her face flush deeply.

"Claudia, it's nothing that you should feel ashamed of. Your father should, but he figures he's privileged, so he never will."

Claudia replied in a broken whisper, "I'm just embarrassed for my poor mother. I think she's suspected for a long time, but has only just learned the truth."

"So now she has to face it."

"Yes. But, she's still trying to make excuses for him, and since I haven't seen anything change around the house, it doesn't seem like she's going to make an issue of it. I can't understand how she copes. I think I'd be out of there in two seconds."

"There's no accounting for how people react in such situations, especially when they have so much to lose."

Claudia looked at Barbara. "You're right. She does have a lot to lose. We all do. But I have a whole life I need to take charge of, and I'm tired of letting other people have so much of a say over it. I didn't even want this job, but my dad talked to Mr. Emerson— senior, not Nathan—and got him to make the job offer. And then, ever since I got the job, my folks have been hinting to me what an eligible bachelor Nathan is. Really, I think they just want me to make a good match so they can call me finished. It's so messy after all, having children who aren't yet settled."

"You have a younger sister too, don't you?"

"Yes." Claudia smiled. "And she has even more of life to figure out. Poor kid."

"You'll be doing her a favor by striking out on your own and making your own decisions. It's awfully hard to rebel when your older sister has always been such a good girl."

"You sound like you're speaking from experience!" Claudia looked at Barbara questioningly.

"Yes!" Barbara gave a short bitter laugh. "Someday I'll tell you that story. Needless to say, it's hard being the younger sibling."

Claudia stood up and took one of the boxes in her arms. "Would you help me with this?"

"I'd be happy to." Barbara reached for the remaining carton on the floor. As they reached the door, she added, "I do think you should talk to Nathan's father. You know this isn't the first time this has happened."

"No, I didn't know." Claudia pushed the door open with her elbow. "I sure wish that someone had told me."

"I wasn't sure it was a pattern, and it seemed like gossiping. Besides I didn't know the other woman as well, so I wasn't ever that clear about what had really happened. But now that I know, I want your story to be told so that he can't ignore it any more."

✷ ✷ ✷

The interview with the senior Mr. Emerson was uncomfortable for Claudia, but Barbara accompanied her, and directed the whole conversation. Mr. Emerson was regretful that Claudia was leaving, and even offered to transfer her to another group, but she was determined to leave.

"I'm leaving to go back to school, Mr. Emerson. I didn't really belong here anyway."

He finally accepted her resignation, while also promising that his son would be disciplined harshly.

Though the afternoon was not over yet, Claudia did not feel like sitting at her desk looking for busy work. She didn't want to run into Nathan again either, so she took her purse and walked out of the building.

She wanted to call Andi and Naomi before she left town, but she couldn't see any reason to tell anyone beyond them. So she made a couple of phone calls and headed over to the Grill to reserve their favorite booth. Within a half hour the three of them were ensconced in the back corner of the restaurant, and Claudia was relating to her friends the events of the last few days. She didn't hold anything back. Somehow she had an uncontrollable need to share it all, so that they would understand why she was leaving and not hold it against her.

"Claudia," Naomi said sympathetically, reaching for her hand. "I'm so sorry. I wish I had known what was going on. Maybe I could have helped in some way."

Claudia's eyes began to smart, even though she hadn't felt weepy until now. "Thanks, Naomi. It feels good just to hear you say it. I think I'm going to cry."

Andi patted her on the shoulder and said, "I think you've handled things very well. What can anyone expect, anyway? You can't solve everybody else's problems. There are just too many of them."

Claudia laughed. "You do have a way of saying things the way you see them!" Then she sighed. "I'm just sad things didn't turn out better with Jeff. But I know he can't just up and move to another state. He has his career. He's all established. Right? Isn't he?"

"Well, yeah. That's the way I was looking at it." Andi said slowly. "But I've been thinking…he's young. People do move around sometimes. And there are always things a good craftsman like Jeff can do to get re-established if he does move. He can work for someone else for a while. He can go through friends to get introduced to contractors who always appreciate having someone skillful to call on."

Claudia didn't want to be too hopeful. "Well, I'm leaving. If he really wants me, he'll have to tackle all those issues."

"Hey Claudia," Naomi reached to pick up her handbag. "I have to get going. I'm sorry, but I'm meeting Ted for dinner."

"Oooh, Ted." Andi grinned widely. "How are things going with Ted?"

Naomi smiled happily. "Very well, Andi. I'm grateful to you for introducing us."

Claudia got up to hug her good bye. "I'm glad you like him and that he likes you back. You do seem very well suited."

"I agree. We have so much in common. And he's so sweet and thoughtful."

"Write to me."

"I will, Claudia. You come back for a visit now and then. I don't care what your parents say. You can always stay with me." Naomi left.

Claudia and Andi sat and picked at their food a little longer before Claudia said sadly, "I'll miss you Andi. You can come visit me too, I hope you know."

"Sure, that would be fun. And you be strong. Okay?"

Claudia gave Andi an uncertain smile. "Sure." She hugged her too and headed home.

* * *

Claudia shut herself in her room so she could pack without anyone interfering or trying to argue her out of her decision to leave. Except for running up and down to do laundry, she did not venture out for the rest of the evening. She felt lonely and forgotten as she folded her clothes and placed them back in the suitcase that she had pulled them out of just a few short weeks earlier.

Even though she had managed to reconnect with Andi and Naomi and felt secure with their friendship, she knew that they were happy in their adult lives already. Both of them had good jobs that suited them, and both of them were in relationships that could lead to something more serious as time went on. Andi and Stewart really seemed to fit together well. The two of them were happy, fun-loving people and had a good set of friends who helped fill their lives. Claudia felt a pang of jealousy as she remembered them together the other night at Andi's apartment, with their gentle touches and glances across the room. They didn't have to talk much to be on the same wavelength.

Claudia's friends would be fine. She knew they cared about her, but they wouldn't suffer if she were gone again. As for her family, she mostly felt bad about leaving Zoë. She really could use the support and guidance of an older sister. But Claudia couldn't live Zoë's life for her. The best she could do is to be a sounding board for her, and with telephones and internet chat, she could just as easily do that from college as she could from her bedroom down the hall. At least Claudia tried to tell herself that. She hoped that it was true. She'd do her best to call Zoë more often—maybe every other day. Maybe even every day. Yes, that could make a difference in her sister's life.

The self-pity grew as she placed her clean clothes into her suitcase. She knew everyone else would survive her absence. She tried to be glad about that, but it would almost be a comfort to her if someone said that her leaving would create an irreparable hole in the universe. The more she brooded, the closer she came to finally admitting that what she would really like was for Jeff to run back to her and pledge to follow her wherever she should go.

But he wasn't going to do it. He had his job here, and he was good at it, and quite well established. She couldn't expect him to leave all that when she wasn't even sure where she would be in a few years. Besides, what was she leaving for, but to go find herself? To spend her time digging in the dirt, and fooling around with clay pots and arrow heads. She knew she wasn't being fair to herself. There were plenty of people in the world who were serious, successful adults who loved the work she wanted to do. But it was times like these when her father's voice came out of her own head to make her feel insignificant. She knew that was another part of why she was leaving—to get out of her father's circle of influence. To get away from her family, when they had nothing but needs and demands to offer her.

Why would Jeff want to leave his life just to help her do that? Better to forget about him and get out of town. She stuffed the last handful of socks into her suitcase and pushed it closed.

She carried it down the stairs to begin packing her car back up with the belongings she had so recently moved home with. Luckily, much of it was still in boxes, so all she needed to do was carry it outside yet again. She had just taken one load out and then headed back in for another when she realized that she was not alone. Her mother had just come into the kitchen in time to see Claudia go down the stairs for another box. *Darn. So much for sneaking out in the dead of night.*

"May I help you?"

Claudia startled, but then nodded and handed her a box. A clattering on the stairs signaled Zoë's presence. Again, Claudia's heart sank at the thought of disappointing her sister, but Zoë wordlessly grabbed another one of Claudia's boxes and struggled up the stairs with it. In no time, all of Claudia's belongings were outside on the driveway ready to be packed into the car.

"Hey, I'm pretty good at Tetris," called her brother from the door.

The much needed laughter released the tension of the moment. Claudia held the keys up for Benjamin to take and stood back waiting for him to take control. With so much help, and with Benjamin's geometric and spatial skills, it didn't take long before everything had been squeezed into the trunk, leaving even more space in the car than Claudia had made for herself on the trip home.

The job done, they locked the car and went into the kitchen for their last bowl of ice cream.

✳ ✳ ✳

Jeff was sitting at the bar having a beer and a Reuben sandwich for lunch when Andi and Stewart came striding in.

"There you are!" Andi exclaimed, heading his way. "Come and sit with us while we discuss the state of the world."

"I'm not sure I'm in the mood to talk about everyone else's problems," Jeff resisted, "since I can't even solve my own."

"Well, it's your own fault really." Stewart grabbed Jeff's arm, and nearly made him fall, pulling him off his stool.

"What?" Jeff was incensed. "What did I do?"

"Come sit with us and you'll find out."

Jeff growled, but he grabbed his beer and his food and followed them to a table in the back corner. Andi must really have something on her mind. Usually she liked to be in the middle of the bar where she could see everything.

"Okay, I'm here."

Do you want to start?" Stewart said to Andi.

"What do you mean start?" Jeff exclaimed. "Just talk to me. What's going on?"

"This is an intervention." Andi said forcefully. "You just sit right there while we straighten you out."

"What's there to straighten out? I thought Claudia made her choice."

"Yes, she did. But you could be a little more supportive, you know.'

"What do you mean supportive? She's leaving me. I'm watching her go. What else can I do?"

Andi and Stewart both looked at Jeff then at each other in mock exasperation. Finally Stewart said, "You're such an idiot."

Jeff half rose from his chair. He was of a mind to pour his entire beer on Stewart's head, but he didn't want to waste it.

Andi giggled and patted Jeff on the hand. "Just sit down, lover boy. You're dense, it's true."

Jeff's anger began to fade. "You mean, there's still some hope for me?"

"Of course there is." Andi smiled broadly. "She's really in love with you, but you really have messed things up."

"But, what…"

"Just listen to Andi." Stewart advised him.

"All right, but you'd better start making sense soon." Jeff tried to glare, but the echo of those words, *She's in love with you!* made it hard for him not to smile.

"Claudia got a call from her favorite professor at college. She was apparently a really good student, and this teacher was really disappointed that she didn't go on to graduate school."

"I know this story already. What's new here? And why didn't she go to graduate school in the first place? I can't understand that."

"Shut up, man."

Jeff shut up.

"Okay, I'll back up. Claudia was supposed to go to college and find a rich, smart, husband to settle down with. When she finished but didn't have a man, her father insisted that she come home and go to work. I have a theory that he meant for her to work at his office all along because he wanted her to end up with Nathan. Nathan's just like Claudia's dad, you know. A real go-getter, thinks he's God's gift to the world and to women especially."

"Well he does seem to have it all," Jeff said glumly. "He's a lawyer, for Pete's sake. He's got education. And he's rich. You can tell just by his clothes."

"But Claudia does not love him," Andi repeated. "That sort never could attract a person like Claudia. She needs someone genuine. Someone real. And she needs someone who needs her. And that's where you have screwed up."

Jeff furrowed his brow. "I don't get it. What did I do? I was as nice to her as I could be! Didn't I show her a good time?"

"Of course you did. And she loves you for it." Andi patted his hand. "But have you told her how much you love her? Have you told her that you *need* her in your life?"

Jeff looked up at Andi. "Well, yeah. I proposed! I told her we were meant for each other."

"You told her that she was meant to live with you in your cute little house here in Carlsburg. Why would you want to do that?"

"What are you talking about? You're supposed to be giving me hope!"

"I'm trying to! But think about it. What are you really hoping for?"

Stewart said, "Andi, settle down. Just tell him what you want him to do."

Andi took a breath. "Would it be impossible for you to go with her?"

Jeff closed his mouth in surprise. What a thought. Could he do it?

"I just bought a house."

Stewart interrupted. "You could get a renter."

Jeff thought about that. "Maybe I could. It's a pretty nice house."

Stewart nodded. "Maybe I could live there for a while. My apartment is kind of small, and my lease is up for renewal next month."

"You would do that? You don't really want to move, do you?"

"I don't have that much stuff really, and I like your house. I'd have the guys over and we'd play poker and drink beer and think of you." Stewart grinned.

"And I could count on you to take decent care of the place and fix things if needed. You're a pretty reliable guy, even though you can bug the hell out of a person."

Stewart hooted with laughter. "At least you see my good side now and then."

"Leaving my work would be harder." Jeff got glum again.

"Now you're being negative." Andi scolded. "You're young. And everybody around here loves you. You can get really good recommendations from the contractors you've been working with, and easily get new work wherever you end up."

"That's true." Stewart nodded vigorously.

"And if you ever come back, they will all be thrilled to work with you again. You're good, and they all know it."

"Well, you seem to have it all figured out."

"Yep." Andi nodded with satisfaction.

Jeff scowled as he tried to wrap his head around these new plans his friends had made for his life. He placed his glass back on the table harder than he meant to and then pulled a bill from his pocket, threw it on the table, got up and walked out of the bar without saying another word to Stewart and Andi. They watched him as he disappeared from sight.

＊＊＊

"Where do you think he's going?" Andi asked Stewart.

"I have no idea." Stewart put his hand over Andi's and rubbed her thumb absently with his own. "But, I think we've done everything we can do."

Andi leaned back against Stewart's strong chest, and snuggled her head into his shoulder. "Were you really looking to get out of your apartment, Stew?"

"Not really," he admitted. "But it's true that my lease is almost up."

"Hmm, so is mine."

CHAPTER 21

Saturday morning, early, Claudia placed her suitcases in the trunk of her car and a backpack full of necessary items in the back seat, and went into the kitchen to brew some coffee for the trip. She had planned to stay another day or two before she left, but here she was all packed, and she didn't see any more reason to wait around. She just hoped that she could get out without anyone arguing with her about it. But she was disappointed when Zoë came clumping down the stairs with her own backpack stuffed full. Throwing it on the floor near the back door, Zoë said, "I'm coming with you."

Claudia looked at her in dismay. "Zoë, I'm not sure…"

Just then, their mother, rolling a small suitcase behind her, appeared in the kitchen doorway. "Would you like help driving east, Claudia?"

Claudia looked from her mother to her sister and back again, and then laughed. "It might be fun."

"Woohoo!" Zoë crowed. She grabbed her mother's suitcase and headed out the door to the car.

Claudia's mother poured herself a cup of coffee and leaned against the counter. She was wide-eyed with excitement. "Claudia, I have to tell you—"

"Mom, I'm sorry about—"

"I'm sorry—"

They both stopped. Then her mother went on.

"Darling, it was not your fault. I've avoided knowing the truth far too long. I just couldn't see any way out of my situation. Even though

Women's Liberation happened years ago, I've always been the one to bend and adjust. He was never going to change, and it was better for me to simply pretend it wasn't happening. The worst of it was when I tried to make you and Zoë bend and adjust too. Can you ever forgive me? I feel so stupid."

"Mom!" Claudia cried, and wrapped her arms around her mother. "You did your best. I don't know that I would have done anything different in your situation. But, I sure don't think of you as stupid! I'm just so sorry that my being home caused so much pain for everybody!"

"Well, I'm glad." Zoë declared, as she came flying back into the room. "And I will have some of that coffee on ice with cream, please."

As Claudia hurried to get a large glass down from the cabinet, Zoë went on, "We were not living any kind of life the way we were. Right, Mom?"

Their mother nodded.

"We needed you to shake us up, Claudia. Even Dad needed it. He doesn't know it now, but he'll be better off than before, now that he is going to be forced to accept that he can't go through life bullying everybody else around him."

Benjamin's head peeked around the corner. "I see a bunch of suitcases. Should I assume that all three of you are going?"

"Benjamin," Zoë wailed, "I'm sorry we're leaving you behind!"

"That's okay. I can handle Dad." Benjamin came in and hugged Zoë and then Claudia. "And I really do have a lot of work to do. I'm just going to miss you all. Things have been really hopping around here lately." He grinned widely as he let Claudia go and turned toward his mother.

She took Benjamin's face between her two hands and said, "Benjamin, I am so proud of you. I hope you know that."

Benjamin looked abashed. "You're not disappointed in me for not going to Princeton?"

"Not at all. I'm proud of you for deciding what you want and facing your father's anger to pursue it."

"Me too, Benjamin." Zoë snuggled in to get a hug.

Claudia joined the group hug and they all stood there for a minute.

"Okay, time to roll." Claudia was the first to disengage.

Five more bustling minutes later and the car was backing down the driveway while Benjamin waved from the doorway.

* * *

"Cause we got a mighty convoy
Rockin' through the night.
Yeah, we got a mighty convoy,
Ain't she a beautiful sight?"

Claudia, Zoë, and their mother sang at the tops of their lungs as they rolled down the highway getting farther and farther away from home and the men in their lives. Though Claudia had contacted Donna Spencer before she left, she couldn't help feeling nervous about what she was going to find when she returned to the school she had just left a few short weeks earlier. She also wasn't quite sure what her mother and sister would do once Claudia had found herself an apartment. Were they planning to move in with her? It would be an interesting situation if they were.

The song finished, and the D.J. came back to banter wittily with his sidekick. Claudia turned down the volume. "So, Mom. What are your plans?"

"Plans?" Her mother turned away, suddenly very interested in the scenery outside the window.

"You can't just stay away from home forever. If nothing else, you have to go back someday to retrieve all your possessions. Right?

Zoë groaned from the back seat. "Claudia, you're such a downer!"

"And you can't live forever without money either. You can't just charge everything!"

A small smile played on her mother's lips. "Well, I did make a few changes in my affairs this week."

"What? What did you do?" Claudia cried in surprise.

"I opened up my own account and moved over some funds. Let's just say, I won't run out of money for a while."

"That's good." Claudia was relieved. She would not have to support her mother on her assistantship. "What are you going to do about Dad?"

"I left him a note. I told him that I know everything and that it's over. I'm going to start a new life. Don't worry, I have it all under control."

"Uh, okay. Then, what about Zoë?"

"Yeah, what about Zoë?" came the voice from the rear.

"Do you want to start a new life with me?" their mother asked with a smile.

"Hell, yes!"

Claudia burst into laughter while her mother tried to shush them both and then gave up.

Just then, through the laughter, the sound of a cell phone got their attention.

"Whose is that?" Claudia's mother scrabbled around the floor in front of her, and finally held up Claudia's purse. "Can I dig in here for your phone?"

"Sure, go ahead."

She opened zippers, and dug into the different pockets, and finally held up the phone, but it had stopped ringing. Looking at the screen, she said, "It was Jeff. Shall I ring him back for you?"

"You mean now? I can't talk to him right now."

"He's really such a nice boy."

"Mom! You don't even like him!"

"I've changed my mind. I spent way too much of my life trying to think the way your father did. But, Jeff was so gentle yet strong with my baby the other day. How can I judge him harshly?"

"I'm glad to hear it, but it's too late. I'm going to grad school, and he lives in Carlsburg."

"I think that's a shame."

"Are you saying that I shouldn't go to graduate school?"

"No, but did you even think to ask him to come along with you?"

Claudia opened her mouth and then closed it again. Why hadn't she? "I never thought of that."

"Don't sell yourself short, Claudia. That boy loves you."

Claudia's eyes began to smart. With a broken voice she admitted, "I know, you're right. He proposed, you know."

"I thought so."

"What?" Zoë again poked her head up from the back seat, pulling out her ear buds at the same time. "Proposed? What did you say?"

"I told him no. I'm not quite sure what I said. I said, more or less, that I was sick and tired of men telling me what to do and that I have to run my own life. And he didn't argue with me. So, see? If he really wanted to be with me, he could have said something."

"But you didn't even suggest that he come with you?"

Claudia was suddenly confused. She went back over the conversation in her head. "Probably not."

Claudia's mother sat back, shaking her head. "Claudia, you love him. Don't you think you ought to do whatever you can to keep him?"

"I wasn't thinking straight! I was so angry with Nathan and Dad."

"And you took it out on Jeff. You should call him."

"I'll think about it," Claudia said, and turned the radio up louder to drown out her mother's voice and her own thoughts.

* * *

Jeff was energized as he left the bar after talking with Stewart and Andi. But driving home, he found himself rethinking that last conversation with Claudia and feeling less certain. Andi seemed so sure that Claudia loved him. He could believe now that the boss's son wasn't going to win her. But she was still leaving town. She had big ambitions—as if he didn't! It hurt to replay her rejection. He hadn't asked her to throw her goals out the window.

Could it be that he was afraid that she didn't see him as ambitious enough? Or was that how Jeff saw himself? And maybe that's why he hadn't tried to cross her father back when he had told Jeff to back off—that Claudia had better things to do than to get herself tied up with him. Maybe because, as hard as he worked, and as respected as he was among his own friends and fellow tradesmen, he really didn't think he was worthy of Claudia.

Suddenly, he was in his driveway staring at the garage door and he knew he didn't want to go inside and wait anymore for happiness to come his way. He knew what he wanted, and she was right within his reach. Damn it! He was honest, brave, strong. His skills earned a good wage. He could make power course safely through metal to light up and warm people's lives. Claudia, her arms welcoming him, her warm soft body yielding to him, was beautiful and smart and good at everything she did. Her talents were totally different from his, but the two of them connected in a special way. They belonged together.

Still sitting in the car, he dug his cell phone out of his pocket and punched in Claudia's number. *Damn, damn, damn.* No answer. Well, if she was going to avoid talking to him, he was just going to make a nuisance of himself until she knew how serious he was about her and how willing he was to change his life for her. Glancing in the mirror, he backed the car out of the driveway again.

✳ ✳ ✳

Jeff parked at the Gilmore home and banged on the door. He tried to decide what he was going to say to Claudia when he saw her. He began to pace back and forth on the stoop. He would propose again, and this time, he wouldn't let her just say no. He would tell her how much he loved her, and that it was fine with him if she wanted to go back to college. That he would go with her, and do whatever she wanted him to do, as long as they could be together. He reached for his pocket and discovered he was still carrying the jewelry box. He knew there was some reason that he hadn't taken that back to the store yet. He turned back to the door with his arm raised to knock again, and—there was Benjamin, leaning against the doorjamb and watching him in amusement.

"You're too late," Benjamin said. "She's left already."

"Left!" Jeff stared at him dumbly.

"Yes. We've had some drama around here in the last few days. She left and took my mom and sister along with her."

"What?" Jeff found himself incapable of saying more than one syllable at a time.

"Yes. She's gone back east. Are you planning on following her? Because if you aren't, I think you won't be seeing her for a really long time."

"Where?" Jeff gulped.

"I can tell you the school and the professor, but no more than that. You'll have to do the rest of the research yourself."

"Thanks." Jeff stood and waited while Benjamin went inside for a pen. Armed with a scrap of paper, Jeff headed home to prepare for a long absence.

CHAPTER 22

After two weeks of being back in the lab, Claudia already felt that she had never left. She would register for a couple of classes once the fall semester began, but for now, most of her responsibilities centered around the research that she had done for her senior project and the other studies going on in the lab. Because she was a research assistant working for a stipend now, she had much more to do than she had had as an undergraduate.

That suited Claudia just fine. Her mother and Zoë had stayed just long enough to help Claudia find and settle into a small but clean rental duplex close to campus. Then she drove them to the local airport so they could fly back to Carlsburg and reorganize their own lives.

"What will you do, Mom?" Claudia had asked as they stood in the airport saying goodbye. "Are you going to forgive Dad?"

"That will depend on him. He's going to have to change. I know one thing for sure—I will never go back to the way things were before. These last two weeks have been so wonderful. I don't quite understand it, but I just feel so free and happy."

Zoë leaned against her mother's shoulder and nodded. "I feel it too, Mom. And I like you so much more when you're not so worried about pleasing Dad."

Claudia laughed. That sister of hers was so perceptive. "And I like you when you're not so busy trying to make Dad mad."

Their mother put her arms around them both. They sat making light conversation until it was time for the two travelers to go through security. Claudia watched them go, trying not to weep openly.

She dove into work in the lab, knowing that if she didn't, she could easily wallow in loneliness. She didn't dare think about Jeff, since it had been so hard to leave him and she was afraid that she would fall into despair. She never did return his call, and he didn't call again, so it became easier and easier to fool herself into thinking that she had made the right decision. *What good would it have done? He would have just made me feel guilty for leaving him again.*

Though she told herself these things, she couldn't get him off her mind. Everywhere she went, she imagined what it would be like to have him near her. When she came home late at night, exhausted from work, while she prepared herself a simple meal of a small salad and a pork chop or a burger, she thought about talking to him about her day. Maybe he would have dinner ready for her some nights, or even take her out to a nice place he had heard about from the guys he worked with. Maybe on her off-days, he would take her for a drive, or they would find a nearby range and go shooting. But why should she wait for him to arrive before she did that herself? She had no idea where there was a range here. And she didn't have her own gun. She'd need to buy one. *How does a person go about buying a gun, anyway?*

Eventually she got fed up with those thoughts and the feeling of helplessness they brought her. She sat down at her computer and started googling gun stores. There was one within a few miles of her apartment, so she printed up the map and early Saturday morning, she set off in her car. Though she had been intimidated just thinking about looking at handguns and trying to decide what to buy for herself, she found a friendly salesman who helped her make sense of it all. Before long she had chosen a .22 caliber revolver that fit her hand perfectly and had a locking carrying case with foam cushions. Three days later, after the obligatory waiting period for purchasing a gun was over, she walked through the parking lot with her new possession in hand and a new confident spring in her step. As she reached her car, she thought she saw a familiar van just pulling into the drive. The driver pulled down his visor right as he passed her, so she didn't see his face, but she could have sworn. . . *But no. It can't be Jeff. I must be losing it.*

Climbing into the car, she drove off. She had a lot to do. Stop imagining things. Jeff is in Carlsburg, not here. You have a new life. Forget about him.

* * *

Several hours later, Claudia's work was done and she was ready to settle down to some dinner and a good book. But suddenly the quiet of the day was interrupted by the sound of a large truck out front. She peered through the window and saw a moving van pulling right up to the duplex next to hers. *Oh no. Just when I was ready for a nice quiet afternoon.* Pulling down the blinds, she resolved to ignore the distraction.

Claudia was surprised at how well she tuned out the noise of the moving operation that was happening on the other side of her living room wall. Even the inevitable thumps and bumps did not cause her to lose her focus on the novel she had resolved to make some progress on before quitting for the night. Finally the noise ended, just as she was coming to the end of a particularly exciting chapter. She was relieved at the silence, since it was time to turn off the lights and go to sleep.

As she lay in bed waiting for sleep to come, her thoughts drifted to Jeff again. She relived the scene in the woods outside Zoë's tent, and the soft kisses that had made her shiver at the time. It made her shiver tonight just thinking about it. She wondered what Jeff would think of her buying her own pistol. Would he be proud? Would he be impressed by her independence? Or would he think she was being silly or worry that she would hurt herself?

She rolled her eyes to herself there in the dark and regained control of her thoughts. She finally fell asleep by going over the statistics that she had run just the day before in her head.

* * *

Jeff lay on his new bed in his new bedroom. He had found this rental place through an online ad. He had worried that it might be a dump or in a bad part of town, but the ad claimed that it was a new building. The rent was reasonable but not overly cheap, so he figured it might not be so bad. Besides, if it was really lousy, he could always give notice and go find something else.

As it turned out, it was a great apartment. The yard was small, but the patio was large enough for some furniture and a grill, which would be nice for an occasional steak or burger. Being in one half of a duplex, he wouldn't have the privacy he was used to in his house in Carlsburg, but it seemed quiet enough.

He was still surprised by the drastic step he had taken. There had been a lot to do to get ready to leave for an extended period of time. But, he had done it all without even knowing what he would find when he got there. When he called on Claudia's mother in the week before he left, she had assured him that, yes, Claudia would be staying in one place for at least four years. She wouldn't give him Claudia's new address, though. He had her cell number. He could call her when he got settled. Then, if she wanted to, Claudia could give him her address and let him see her. He urged Mrs. Gilmore to take his own address, just in case she spoke to Claudia and wanted to share it with her. When she glanced at the paper he handed her, she gave him an amused smile that he didn't understand. But it wasn't important. He was on his way.

With references from several of the contractors that he often worked for, he had no trouble getting in with a couple of builders here. There would easily be enough work for him. He didn't mind the long drive east in his van. It gave him time to think and plan.

He would spend all day tomorrow unpacking and then get to work on Monday. Once he felt settled, he would go search for Claudia. Benjamin had given him the name of her professor. If he couldn't find her any other way, he could just stake out her office until Claudia showed up. He wasn't going to give up—this time.

CHAPTER 23

The next day, Claudia stayed in so as not to bother her new neighbor. She had a lot of reading to do for her research, and then whenever she needed a break from that, she picked up her novel or puttered around the kitchen preparing meals for the coming week.

Monday, Claudia opened her curtains and looked out to see what the weather was going to be that day. Though the sun was bright and the sky was clear, she felt tired and a little bit down. *Dressing up should put me in a better mood.* She spent a little extra time putting on her makeup and choosing her outfit for the day. By nine o'clock she was finally pulling out of the garage and down the driveway.

Before she got onto the road, though, she pulled out her cell phone and dialed Andi.

"Claudia! What's new? How's the job? How's your new apartment? Have you met any cute guys?"

Claudia laughed. It was good to hear Andi's voice. "The job is working out really well. I know I did the right thing to come back here. It's good to be on my own and independent. I feel so much stronger when I'm in charge of my life."

"That's great." Andi's voice sounded a little strange. "So, you haven't met up with anyone special?"

"What? Already?" Claudia was confused. "I just got here. I'm not even interested in meeting men right now. In fact…"

"Jeff?" Andi spoke knowingly.

"I have been thinking about him, yes. It just seems I wish I had everything. I want the perfect work, I want to keep studying, and I want that man."

"Haven't you heard from him at all since you left?"

"Well, to tell you the truth, he did call once while I was driving out here. But I missed it and I haven't had the nerve to call him back."

"And he hasn't called again?"

"No. At least I don't think so. I think he's given up on me."

"Uh. I don't think so. You should call him back."

"I know. Every day I think about it and try to get up the nerve. I don't know what to say."

"Make the call. The rest will fall into place. I promise."

Claudia laughed nervously. "Okay. Maybe that will give me the oomph I need. I'll let you know."

"Good. Do that. Hey, I gotta get back to work. I'll talk to you later."

Claudia said good-bye. She pulled into her parking space at her building and sat in the car for a while. Finally she shook herself and decided to think about Jeff later. For now though, it was time to get to work. Before sticking the cell phone back into her purse, she quickly scrolled through the recent calls. Yes, there was Jeff's phone number. She would call him back. Soon.

✳ ✳ ✳

When Claudia returned home that night, she glanced over at the other side of the duplex. The garage door was closed and the blinds drawn, so she couldn't see inside, but she figured that her new neighbor was home, because there was a new potted plant out on the step. She smiled to see that the place would be well taken care of.

She went inside her own apartment and left her purse by the front door. On second thought, she leaned over to take her cell phone out of her purse and laid it on the kitchen counter. This way, she could brood over it while she had her dinner. Throughout her meal and the cleanup afterward, she thought about what to say to Jeff. She didn't blame him for not calling again. He could probably only take so much, and then he had to assume that yet again, she had decided that she was too good for the likes of him.

She couldn't put it off any longer. She knew that the time back in Carlsburg was one hour earlier, but it was eight o'clock here, and he really should be home.

She lifted the phone from the counter and scrolled through her contacts until she found his number. She hit call and waited. One ring. Suddenly, she heard a familiar ringtone through the wall of her living room from the direction of her new neighbor. Her cell rang again. Then the ring on the other side of the wall also sounded. After the third ring, Jeff's voice came on the line.

"Claudia?"

"Jeff? Where are you?"

"Umm, I'm at home. What's up?"

Claudia frowned at the wall. "I've been thinking about you. Jeff, I miss you."

"I miss you too. Why did you have to leave so suddenly?"

"I had to go, Jeff. I was so afraid that someone would make me change my mind...my father...you..."

"I'm sorry, Claudia."

"Why are you sorry?" Claudia was beginning to cry softly. "You didn't do anything wrong. It was me. I left you the first time, and then I left you again and never gave you a chance to—"

"No, you can't take all the blame," Jeff insisted. "I should have realized that you had even less ability to cross your father than I had. I shouldn't have believed him. I should have had faith in you, and in our love."

"Our love?" Claudia sniffed.

"Yes, I love you. I can't let you go."

"But I can't come back. You have to understand, Jeff! I need this for myself. I need to have my own work—something that I love— something that fascinates me and that I'm good at."

"I know, Claudia. I would never make you leave work you love. But..."

"But?"

"But, what do you think about me coming to live near you? We can pick up where we left off—see where things go from there."

＊ ＊ ＊

Now that he got it out, Jeff held his breath. But he couldn't sit still while he waited for Claudia's reply. He jumped up from his seat in the kitchen and banged through the back door to his patio. The space was small but he managed to find a path to pace, back and forth, back and forth.

＊ ＊ ＊

Claudia found herself speechless. Jeff had offered, without her needing to prod him, to leave his whole life behind and follow her. Somewhere in the rear of the house she heard a door open and then slam. And then, through the phone, she heard the same sounds. *There is something very strange going on!*

She moved to the back door as quietly as she could, slipped through it and across the lawn to the end of the brick wall separating her yard from the one next door. As she slowly peeked around the corner, Jeff was reaching the opposite end of his porch and swung around. His eyes met hers. In her surprise, Claudia gasped, clutched her cell phone to her chest, and then withdrew to her own side of the wall. Jeff saw her but couldn't move from his spot. He was holding on to his own phone so hard, waiting for her to speak again. Finally realizing that she wasn't going to speak any more, he ran around the wall to face her and grabbed her by the shoulders.

"How did you find me?" He asked at the same time that she cried out,

"Are you stalking me?"

"What?" "I didn't!" "Of course not!"

Suddenly she was crying and hugging him, and he was covering her face with kisses. Claudia couldn't believe the feeling of relief that washed over her. Soon she was kissing him back and laughing with tears running down her face. "No wonder Andi sounded so strange on the phone earlier today, asking me if I hadn't heard from you lately."

"And why your mother looked at me so funny when I gave her my new address."

She grabbed his hair and pulled his mouth down to hers. He covered her mouth with his own. This time the kiss lasted a good long time.

✳ ✳ ✳

Finally, Jeff allowed himself to release his hold on Claudia. She felt so good in his arms—so soft, so yielding, yet so insistent and demanding.

"Come into my house. I have something to show you."

Once in the living room, he offered her a glass of her favorite white wine. He then led her to the sofa and offered her a seat.

"And now that you are completely relaxed—you are, aren't you?" At her nod, he continued. "I have a question I want to ask you again."

"Go ahead."

Jeff brought his hand into view. It contained the small box that Claudia had seen before but hadn't looked at very carefully. He opened it slowly, and this time she really looked inside. It contained a lovely gold ring with a simple, brilliant-cut diamond, framed by several smaller diamonds on each side. Claudia caught her breath.

"Will you marry me?"

"Yes, yes, yes, I will!"

Jeff took the ring from the box and Claudia held out her hand so he could place it on her finger. Her eyes were brimming with tears as she moved her gaze from the ring to Jeff's face. He had such a look of love in his eyes.

Jeff lowered his head to hers, and they kissed—a soft gentle kiss, this time, not a passionate impatient kiss like before. She knew that there were many sides to this man, and she was looking forward to knowing them all.

About the Author

Rebecca Gray's career as a romance author began after years of reading manuscripts for her many writer friends. But even her childhood buddies recall role playing in her imaginative "People Games," and her three homeschooled children were educated by the stories Rebecca and her true love, Greg, wove to explain psychology, history, and even math.

Rebecca now writes from the comfort of the family home set deep in the woods and along the streams of rural Northern Illinois, at a time in her life when she is finally free to craft her fantasies to her heart's content.